AETHER

J.H. Mills

ENSŌ
STUDIOS

ISBN: 979-8-9987327-1-3

For Jim and Jen.

ACKNOWLEDGMENTS

Thank you to:

My Editor, Fleetwood Robbins. I appreciate your guidance and expertise. You helped me create the strong foundation I needed at the start.

James Paradies and Jennifer Plumley. Your friendship and support over the years has meant the world to me.

Looking Glass Studios, Irrational Games (particularly Ken Levine, whom I had the honor to meet one day), Interplay Productions, and Bethesda Studios. Their games: "Thief", "System Shock" and "Fallout" have been extremely influential in my life. And although this book exists in its own mythology, it owes a debt of gratitude to those amazing game franchises.

The United States and Australian militaries, and the many defense corporations whose innovations keep us safe and competitive on the world stage.

The state of New York, and the Hudson Valley in particular, for being one of many amazing backgrounds of my life.

PROLOGUE

THE DAY OF FIRE

Tomorrow...

Two miles beneath Denver International Airport, the shrill ring of a phone shattered the quiet of Phoenix Central Command Headquarters. The phone was on the desk of the regional director.

"Centcom, this is Beckett." Sam Beckett juggled the handset while putting on his suit jacket. It was Friday afternoon, and he was about to leave for the day.

"It's Bob Meyers from Analytics." He sounded out of breath.

"Meyers, unless it's—" Meyers cut him off.

"It's urgent."

"It better be," said Beckett. "I'm about to go home and have a nice dinner. Can this—"

1

"I'm sorry, sir," said Meyers. "It's Viridian Island. Kicked everything off."

"I thought that was handled by the Navy."

"It was," said Meyers. "We sent you the report. Did you—"

"Yeah, I read it," said Beckett. "SecDef wrote it himself. Made damn sure everyone knew it, too. It read like some kind of...I don't know...1950s sci-fi movie or something."

"It was an Oceanus research team," said Meyers. "I didn't read it all the way through."

"Portal division," said Beckett. "Something came out of one into a lab on the island. They had to nuke the island to contain it."

"Something?"

Beckett ignored the question. "Sent LCAC hovercraft with a bunch of Marines to evacuate," Beckett continued. "They got back to their San Antonio-class LPD and discovered someone was infected."

"Infected? With what?" said Meyers.

"Unknown," said Beckett. "Whatever it was, the MARSOC guys running the evac mission were no match for it. Navy relayed video footage as it was happening. They requested backup, but backup came in the form of a nuclear warhead-tipped torpedo from a Los Angeles-class sub."

"My god..." said Meyers.

"Skipper on the sub was ordered to fire danger close. Now both vessels are at the bottom of the Pacific."

Meyers gasped. "So many people...just...gone."

"Yeah, real tragedy," said Beckett. He was not in a remorseful mood. "So that's it? Problem solved?"

"I'm afraid not," said Meyers. "That's why I'm calling. The Russians and Chinese got involved. There was a series of escalations. Check your email."

Beckett opened his email. There was one unopened message from Meyers. He opened it and scanned down the page.

"Are you sure about this? Run it past Janice?"

"This is from Janice. My team checked it four times. Cross-checked it with our intel connections."

"If this is true," said Beckett. "The Descent is about to begin."

2

"Yes, sir," said Meyers. "As it was foretold. All Hail Columbia."

"Columbia shall rise," said Beckett, responding in kind.

Beckett wasn't a true believer. Phoenix's plans for the future of United States were important, of course. He just didn't buy into the religious mumbo-jumbo. Some did, and to keep morale high, he wanted others to think that he did too. He'd become an expert at faking it.

"Listen, Meyers. If this is true, a lot is about to change, and fast. The Green Book will be our guide, of course, but we may not follow it to the letter. I hope you understand that."

"I've always seen it as aspirational," said Meyers. "I know there are zealots—"

"When the time comes, I hope I can depend on you and your department to be...compliant."

"You can count on us, sir."

"Good," said Beckett. "Our mandate is clear. Once The Descent begins, Central Command is in charge. If East and West don't want to fall in line...well, we're prepared for that."

"But sir, what about the President—" said Meyers. Beckett cut him off.

"Compliant, Meyers."

Meyers was silent. He knew what Beckett was getting at, and he didn't like the implication. His department was resilient, but he was concerned about some of the others. Lives would be lost at the hands of security, he was sure of it. It had happened before, and in less stressful times. He exhaled, closed his eyes, and shook his head...bracing for the inevitable.

A warning klaxon sounded in the hall, and the lights changed to red. There were flashing white lights at the lower corners of several doors, indicating emergency exits.

Beckett pressed the "Acknowledge / Silence" button on his desk. The alarm sound stopped, but the lights in the hallway remained red.

There were screams on Meyers' side of the phone. Beckett heard Meyers cup the phone with his hand and shout something that was too muffled to understand.

A digital sign activated on the wall in Beckett's office. A red title blinked in 72-point Helvetica. Now it was official. Sam Beckett had prepared his whole career for this, and now it was time to go to work. Years of training took over, and his mind was already mapping out the first steps.

"Well," said Beckett. "Looks like it's coming down." He unlocked the bottom right drawer on his desk, pulled out a rare bottle of single malt, and a rocks glass. He exhaled as he poured two fingers for himself.

Beckett paused, thinking for a few seconds. "Send the recall. Recall everyone," he said.

"Everyone?" said Meyers.

"Full distribution. The other commands, too. Tell them they have an hour to get here before we lock the place down."

"And if they don't?"

"Not our problem," said Beckett. "East and West probably won't come anyway. Well, some might...the devout. Most will shelter in place. Listen, call an emergency meeting with the department heads. Fifteen minutes. Main conference room."

"Yes, sir."

"Keep your department calm," said Beckett. "This is gonna be a stressful time for everyone. And, uh...if you have anyone to call, do it now. But do it quietly. No need to panic the others. I'm hanging up now."

Beckett dropped the handset into its receiver. The recall was about to be sent, and the clock was ticking. Beckett paused for a moment, letting the gravity of the situation settle over him. The weight of it pressed down on him like a lead blanket.

The Descent. Decades of secrecy and preparation, and now it was here. Phoenix would rise from the ashes, and so would its new nation: Neo-Columbia. But first, they had to save some important people.

***

Twenty minutes later...

Fifteen Dassault Falcon 10X jets landed in quick succession at a private airstrip just east of Fort Knox Army Base in Kentucky. The jets bore no markings except for their tail numbers, operating under military-level restricted flight plans. For all intents and purposes, they didn't exist—not on FAA records and not on radar.

Flanking each jet were two sleek, delta-shaped stealth drones. Their surfaces shimmered faintly in the fading sunlight, equipped with advanced optical camouflage. These machines were invisible to most forms of electronic detection, and when necessary, to the human eye. Each was armed with an arsenal of ballistic and coherent light weapons, and had missiles capable of neutralizing just about anything on a modern battlefield.

Ground crews moved with precision as the jets taxied into position. The instant engines powered down, passengers were ushered out by their escorts—heavily armed BlackJack security teams, their dark-gray polo shirts adorned with the unmistakable red trident logo.

The airstrip was locked down like a fortress. Layers of security formed three concentric circles around the perimeter. Radar-guided Phalanx guns, anti-aircraft missile batteries, and sniper teams on elevated platforms ensured nothing came near the operation unnoticed—or unchallenged.

Inside the jets, the passengers represented the elite of the elite: the families of the Board of Trustees of Ouroboros. This was no ordinary private equity firm. Ouroboros owned nothing, produced nothing, and needed nothing. Its purpose was singular: control. Through its three dominant investment firms—BlackRaven, SuperColossus, and Nation Street—it held trillions of dollars in assets, influencing every major industry, government, and critical infrastructure across the globe.

As the passengers disembarked, they were hurried into a nearby hangar, escorted past towering steel walls reinforced with layers of composite armor. In the center of the cavernous space, a massive cargo elevator awaited. Its gleaming steel walls bore Ouroboros's insignia: a minimalistic, abstract serpent devouring its tail, symbolizing endless renewal and the unyielding cycle of power.

The elevator doors slid open, revealing a chamber large enough to fit several tractor-trailers side by side. Once the last passenger was aboard, BlackJack operatives took up defensive positions around the hangar. A tense silence fell over the space as the elevator began its descent, the hum of industrial machinery echoing faintly in the background.

The descent lasted ten minutes. When the elevator doors finally opened, it revealed an underground logistics terminal unlike anything the passengers had ever seen. Bright floodlights illuminated a vast railyard, where polished tracks gleamed like silver veins running across the ground in all directions.

A sleek blue train waited at the platform, its mirrored surface gleaming. The wide double doors stood open, and two imposing guards flanked the entrance, their presence even more unnerving than the BlackJack escorts left behind on the surface.

A man stepped forward to greet them. He was middle-aged, unremarkable in appearance, with neatly combed brown hair, glasses, and a trimmed mustache. His dark brown suit was perfectly pressed, and his demeanor radiated calm professionalism. If there was a word to describe him, it would be disarming.

"Welcome," he said with a warm smile, his voice smooth and reassuring. "Please, step inside and take any seat you like. If you require anything, don't hesitate to ask."

The passengers hesitated for a moment, but then the group began moving toward the train. The man stood to the side, hands clasped in front of him, watching as they boarded.

"That's the train's A.I.," said one of the passengers, his voice low as he addressed the woman beside him. "Not a real person."

"What?" the woman asked, clutching his arm as her eyes darted around nervously.

"It's a soligram," he explained. "A projection made of nanotech particles. Watch this."

The man reached out and waved his hand through the greeter's midsection. His fingers passed through effortlessly, scattering tiny flecks of light and matter that quickly reassembled themselves.

The greeter turned toward the woman and smiled, entirely unfazed. "Mind the gap," he said pleasantly.

"The…gap?" she stammered, blinking in confusion.

"Between the platform and the train, ma'am."

"Oh! Yes, of course." She laughed nervously and stepped into the train, still clutching her companion's arm. He began explaining nanotech aerostat soligrams in a hushed voice as they found their seats.

When the last passenger had boarded, the guards at the entrance exchanged a glance and a nod.

A tug on his pant leg drew the male guard's attention. He looked down to find a little girl, no older than six or seven, staring up at him with wide, curious eyes.

"Are you real?" she asked.

The guard's face softened as he slung his weapon over his shoulder and knelt down to her level. "Of course I'm real. What kind of question is that?"

"My mom said you weren't."

He chuckled. "Well, your mom's mistaken. I have a mom and dad, just like you."

"Where are you from?"

"Philadelphia," he said, his tone light. "That's in Pennsylvania. Do you know Pennsylvania?"

The girl nodded slowly. "You have really pretty eyes."

"Thank you," he replied, smiling warmly.

"Athena!" a woman called from inside the train. "Come on, sweetie, we found seats."

The little girl ran back to her mother, but not before glancing over her shoulder one last time. The guard gave her a reassuring wink. For a brief moment, his irises glowed a bright, unnatural green. The girl's jaw dropped in amazement just as the train doors closed.

***

To: All Phoenix Personnel
From: Phoenix CentCom
Subject: CRITICAL | SEVERITY 1 | RECALL - Seek Shelter Immediately
Message Follows:
Attention all Phoenix Personnel,
This is NOT a test. A series of global events have resulted in a critical

breakdown of international diplomacy—world war is imminent.

OPLAN 8010-24 is now in place. Gold Codes have been received and verified. Level-4 SKYKING emergency action messages have been intercepted on various military HF frequencies. Authentication "X-RAY ZULU" has been confirmed via DIA.

The Pentagon has changed our posture to DEFCON 1, and NORAD reports angels inbound. Time to first impact is estimated at less than one hour.

Action Required:

Return to Central Command headquarters immediately. If you are unable, shelter in place at a regional HQ or your closest facility. If you are above ground, make every effort to get to your nearest Phoenix location. All surface locations are considered compromised.

Take immediate action, stay calm, and await further instructions.

***

Fifty-seven minutes later...

The surface of the Earth became fire, radiation, and death. Hundreds of nuclear missiles rained down on the United States. An overburdened missile defense system stopped only eleven percent. Many warheads were cobalt-salted, their deadly legacy lingering for centuries. In other parts of the world, it was worse. Entire continents became graveyards. Forests turned to ash, and the oceans boiled with the silent screams of dying marine life.

People in towns and cities across the globe scrambled for solace. In their final moments, some whispered desperate prayers, others clutched their children, and many simply ran out of time. In Sioux Falls, South Dakota, a grandmother threw herself over her granddaughter as the blast of a 20-megaton airburst reduced them to shadows on the wall. They were gone before they could feel the heat or comprehend the light.

Yet amidst the annihilation, New York state clung to a fragile thread of salvation. Lerna, a prototype defense system nicknamed "The Hydra," stood vigilant. A lattice of 100 high-energy kill-shot lasers,

Lerna had been derided as a multi-billion-dollar boondoggle at the Pentagon. But on that day, it lived up to its mythic name. Despite a cascade of malfunctions and misalignments, it obliterated every missile destined for the Empire State.

Victory, however, was an illusion. Survivors emerged from shelters, blinking in disbelief at a skyline untouched by warheads. But the air itself carried death. Radioactive fallout swept in from neighboring regions, blanketing the state in a lethal shroud. The invisible poison invaded their bodies, sealing their fate. New York's infrastructure stood defiant, but its people faced the same grim end as the rest of the world. The Hydra had slain its enemies, but the war was over, and humanity had lost.

***

700 years later...

A satellite in geosynchronous orbit took snapshots of North America. It was kept in service by a small army of automated maintenance drones, most of which were now non-functional. In one of the satellite's images, a small pocket of green showed bright against an ocean of gray and brown. If one zoomed in on this high-resolution image, they would see the area formerly known as New York's Hudson Valley.

The satellite's diagnostic software examined the image and detected several anomalies. The terrain did not quite line up with its onboard maps, and there was an issue in the lower-right quadrant. A patch of uniform gray obscured part of the landscape. The software cross-referenced the area in its database and got a hit. It added annotations and metadata, then encrypted the image and broadcast it as directed.

Its work was almost in vain. The stations the message was intended for were long out of service. But the image was received, decrypted, and viewed—just not by its intended audience.

A bright yellow border surrounded the image. At the top-left, in bold red, was written: TOP SECRET//SCI. Below that: NEW YORK - ULSTER AND DUTCHESS COUNTIES. At the bottom-left, there was a black, circular logo of a bird in flight. Under that, the word PHOENIX. An outline of the map of New York is superimposed over the satellite imagery.

In the lower-left section of the area outlined as Dutchess County is the city of Poughkeepsie. It is covered in a dark gray cloud. The cloud's outer rim is a lighter shade of gray and denser. The image's metadata concerning this area reads:

Access Level: Ravenor or Higher

1.1.1.9.5 - Call Sign: Eternal Taiga

Active Security Detected - Type: Aether - Security Posture: Defense (3 of 5)

Additional active command systems detected:

Miasma: psychological warfare package.

Renascent: control and coordination package.

Renascent has the following active cells:

REAPER [human remains] (count: 57)

Program: Perimeter Defense - Hunt and Kill Formation

Location: Poughkeepsie Rural Cemetery

Warning: Three REAPER units contain malfunctioning Archimedes mesh network processors. Uncontrolled units may display erratic behavior and/or present an extreme threat.

Summary: Facility 1.1.1.9.5 [Eternal Taiga] is under active defense but is not connected to DefenseNet. Troop white-listing is not possible at this time. Friendly units are advised to stay clear of the area.

***

The satellite received, negotiated, and accepted an encrypted connection from a trusted terrestrial station. The satellite was put into manual control mode. The main visible light camera was switched to live video, and then zoomed in toward the Poughkeepsie area. It came to rest over a slowly swirling gray cloud, which lay like a blanket over the city.

A pulsating red light on top of a radio antenna poked out of the cloud. The camera centered on it, then panned west, across the Hudson

River, to a large opening in a wooded area. A group of buildings was surrounded by an impressive stone wall. The main building was a large square made of large stone blocks. It had towers on each corner and a square courtyard in the center.

It was dusk, giving everything a yellow-orange tint. Long shadows extended from the structures in view. Based on their length, the satellite determined that the main building was three stories tall, its towers an additional three.

The camera zoomed in and centered on the main building's roof. A woman with short black hair was there, hunched over, hands on her knees, her breathing labored. She had a thin, athletic build, and was dressed in a dark form-fitting outfit with a utility belt. The satellite calculated her height at about 5 feet, 10 inches, or 178 centimeters.

The woman glanced at the horizon as if expecting trouble. Something caught her attention. She moved toward the edge of the roof in a smooth, semi-crouch with the stealth and grace of a hunting cat.

The satellite's camera shifted off the woman, tracking east in the direction of her gaze, and came to rest on the compound's gatehouse. Two large doors swung inward, and a group of twenty to thirty men ran inside. Many were dressed in metal plate armor and had swords in their hands.

ACT I - THE KINGDOM OF YORKE

1

A mischievous shadow moved in the patchy, pre-dawn fog outside Cushing Cottage. She'd planned this job for days, carefully watching staff rotations and guard patrols.

Ella Wellington wore her best thieving gear, well broken-in and slightly faded—just the way she liked it. Whisper quiet, she blended seamlessly into any reasonably dark shadow.

She reviewed her map and notes. Cushing Cottage had been a military outpost and was built like a fortress. The lower levels were heavily fortified; all first and second-floor entrances were sealed from the inside or protected by heavy wrought-iron bars. She would have to climb the cottage's outer stone wall and enter through a third-story bedroom window—a standard infiltration route she'd used countless times.

Following her planned path, she scaled the wall effortlessly and slipped into a dark bedroom. The cool, stale air indicated this room was seldom occupied. Her target lay on the second floor, and her escape route would lead down to the ground floor, exiting through any available side entrance.

She stepped cautiously into the hallway, muffling her footsteps on a luxurious carpet runner. The cottage's interior was lavishly decorated in a style befitting a Countess, though Ella privately considered it gaudy. Heavy brocade curtains hung beside tall, leaded-glass windows, tied back with braided gold cords. Dark polished oak walls displayed ornate paintings of the kind of people she hoped she'd never meet.

Ella's gaze flicked disdainfully to a large, gilded chandelier overhead. Gaslights cast long, wavering shadows over gilded mirrors and intricate tapestries. She grimaced at the excessive gold leaf accents on furniture and frames.

She turned onto a grand staircase that swept elegantly downward, its polished mahogany banisters gleaming excessively. Halfway down, Ella paused; a guard stood at the landing, scratching under his collar. She crept silently behind him, blackjack ready, but at the last moment, he sighed and wandered off toward the east wing.

Ella exhaled slowly, stowing her blackjack and moving onward to the second-floor gallery. Marble pedestals lined the corridor, displaying statues and vases—more unnecessary wealth, she thought bitterly.

Ahead, prominently displayed on a carved pedestal inside a protective glass case, lay her treasure. She swiftly opened the case, carefully grasping the handmade object, savoring its fine texture.

Footsteps approached from the next room. She quickly hid the object in her sack and closed the case door, retreating to the nearest shadowy corner. A guard entered, silhouetted by hallway lights, heading directly toward the display.

"What the!" The guard rubbed his chin. "Hmmm… I thought there was…"

Ella slipped unnoticed through the open door behind him.

"Probably being cleaned," he muttered as she vanished.

Her mission complete, Ella descended to the first floor via a dim service staircase. Staff were active here, forcing her to wait patiently before dashing through an exterior door into the courtyard. Dawn air crystallized dew into frost, shimmering briefly in the emerging sunlight.

Smiling, Ella hummed contentedly, entering her modest domicile. Breakfast awaited, laid out neatly. She lowered her hood, inhaling the aroma appreciatively. She set her prize—a small doll with black yarn hair, a blue dress, and button eyes—on the table against a candlestick. Nearly worthless monetarily, it was priceless to Ella.

"Have a good night, ma'am?" asked a familiar voice.

Ella sprang up, dagger drawn instinctively.

A smiling Mrs. Baybridge emerged from the shadows.

"For fuck's sake," Ella groaned. "Mrs. Baybridge, you've missed your calling."

"Have I?" Baybridge replied, clearly delighted.

"Not many can sneak up on me," Ella admitted.

"Oh, indeed?"

"No," Ella confirmed, sitting back down and sheathing her dagger. "But before I forget myself, thank you for breakfast."

"Yes, ma'am." Baybridge gestured toward the doll. "Speaking of forgetting yourself, Countess, why exactly are you sneaking around your own home and stealing your own property?"

Ella sighed, biting her toast. "I'm not doing well with retirement."

"I can see that. You don't even stay in your own house?"

"I feel more comfortable here," Ella explained. "The Cottage is too big—too much open space."

"I understand," Baybridge softened, adopting a maternal tone. "You've been here just over a month. A transition period is understandable. Your previous job was exciting; from what I hear."

"You could say that," Ella replied dryly.

"Yorke's Intelligence Corps," Baybridge said approvingly. "And a Commander, no less!"

"Not anymore," Ella corrected her. "And I'm not sure about the fru-fru title either."

"The noble rank is an honor," Baybridge pointed out gently. "Few earn it; many die trying."

"I don't mean disrespect," Ella said quickly.

Baybridge smiled. "If adventure is what you miss, explore outside the grounds. Plenty to see from the old world—before the Day of Fire."

"Outside the compound, huh?"

"It's not a compound. You're not imprisoned here. But consult Captain Shelling first; monsters have been sighted nearby."

Ella nodded. "Thank you, I'll consider it."

"Yes, ma'am." Baybridge withdrew.

***

Countess Ella Wellington strode confidently toward the front gatehouse. The sun was higher now, gently pushing back the last traces of dawn chill around Cushing Cottage. Yet within Gloamwood, thick mist stubbornly clung to the ground, swirling slowly through the trunks of ancient, gnarled trees. Occasional bright shafts of sunlight pierced the dense canopy above, spotlighting the eerie scene below.

The gatehouse buzzed with activity as guards moved briskly, attending to their morning tasks. Seeing Ella approach, several guards paused, offering polite nods or respectful salutes.

"Good morning, ma'am," said a young guard stationed at the gatehouse entrance. "Looking for someone?"

"Indeed," she replied. "Please fetch Captain Shelling for me."

The guard quickly complied, disappearing into the gatehouse and returning moments later with Mr. Shelling, Captain of the Guard. Shelling was a broad-shouldered man nearing fifty, with streaks of gray highlighting his close-cropped hair. His eyes carried the sharpness of experience and caution.

"Countess," Shelling greeted, nodding respectfully. "How can I assist you this morning?"

"I intend to explore some ruins beyond the Cottage walls today," Ella explained. "Mrs. Baybridge suggested it might ease my restlessness."

Shelling frowned slightly, shaking his head. "I admire your spirit, Countess, truly—but Gloamwood isn't safe lately. There have been sightings of creatures large enough to threaten entire patrols."

Ella smiled. "Gloamwood?"

Shelling nodded, eyes narrowing. "Yes. Old name, from before the Day of Fire. The woods grew strange after...changed, they say. It's beautiful, but deadly."

"I'm familiar with danger, Captain. You know that," she said gently.

"No question," Shelling conceded. "But humor me. Take two of my men at least, if only to keep me from worrying myself into an early grave."

Ella laughed warmly. "All right. Two guards, if you insist."

Minutes later, she exited the compound gates accompanied by two young guards. They were strong and eager, stepping briskly as they entered the shadowed paths of Gloamwood. Shafts of sunlight shifted and danced around them, casting unsettling shapes across their path.

"An honor to escort you, Countess," said the first guard, a sandy-haired youth named Finn. "We've heard so many stories."

"Yes," added the second, slightly shorter but sturdily built, named Bran. "They say you're unstoppable. Like the time you freed all those prisoners from Cragscliff prison."

Ella shook her head, amused yet melancholy. "Exaggerations, I'm afraid. It was only one prisoner. And... she didn't make it out alive. A terrible loss, and one I deeply regret. I managed to recover her intel, and command called it a victory. But it wasn't. Not for me."

The two guards exchanged an uneasy glance. Bran pressed further, hesitant but curious. "What about the time you stole the ring right off the King of Saug's finger? Everyone talks about it."

Ella chuckled softly. "Oh, that one's true—but it's not as glamorous as it sounds. The king was drunk, asleep in his chambers, and guarded only by incompetence. Hardly a daring feat."

Finn grinned, clearly delighted to confirm at least one of the legendary stories. "But it changed the course of the negotiations, didn't it?"

"It did," Ella admitted. "Though I'd prefer diplomacy over thievery, given the choice."

They fell quiet as they reached a cluster of ruins—a long-abandoned strip mall. An overgrown parking lot stretched out before them, weeds and grass pushing through cracked pavement. Rusting vehicles sat silently, mysterious relics from a forgotten age.

"What are those?" Ella asked, genuinely puzzled as she examined the strange metal objects.

Finn stepped forward, inspecting them closely. "I heard they were private booths. You know, where people sat to eat their food."

Ella raised an eyebrow skeptically. "Strange way to dine."

Nearby stood crumbling storefronts, signs barely readable through centuries of decay. One read "'Merica Diner – Welcome!" next to an abstract American flag faded with age. Another storefront bore a cheerful logo featuring a muscular anthropomorphic bison: "Bison Burg," the sign proclaimed boldly. Beside it, the once-bright colors of "Beanie Supermarket" were now dimmed, the large brown bean logo cracked and weathered.

Suddenly, from somewhere deep within the forest, a low, menacing growl echoed through the trees. Ella's senses sharpened instantly.

"What was that?" Bran whispered urgently, drawing his sword.

Ella stood perfectly still, listening carefully. Another, louder growl reverberated, followed by heavy, rhythmic thuds growing rapidly closer.

"Time to leave," Ella said sharply. "Back to the Cottage. Now."

Finn and Bran fell into defensive positions as they moved swiftly toward safety. Behind them, branches cracked ominously, something massive emerging from the shadows. Ella felt a thrill surge through her veins, familiar yet chilling, as they raced back toward the protection of Cushing Cottage.

***

Countess Ella Wellington climbed out onto the roof of Cushing Cottage, sweaty and breathing heavily from the exertion. She had scaled the outer wall using a decorative, ivy-covered lattice, the exhilarating final obstacle of her "confidence course"—a winding series of climbs and jumps around the property designed to keep her skills sharp.

She paused, heart rate gradually steadying. Closing her eyes, Ella attempted to savor the calming sounds of nature, but instead, distant, rhythmic thumps of siege engines echoed through the valley. Saug was clearly pressing an aggressive advance, the battle lines extending farther south than usual. Over the two decades of intermittent conflict, the front had fluctuated frequently, but always centered around the Ramparts—a fortified, mountainous stretch that divided the Kingdoms of Yorke and Saug. Although Yorke was currently on the defensive, Ella wasn't overly concerned; such ebb and flow had defined her years in intelligence.

Countess turned her face toward the setting sun. Late summer air, laced with wood smoke and pine sap, brushed coolly against her skin. She noted fires being lit below, the gentle murmur of staff preparing for a chilly evening.

Vorpal Vale spread majestically beneath her, bathed in a warm, golden hue. To the east, the Hud river shimmered serenely. Beyond it, the towering, impenetrable cloud wall of the Forbidden Land loomed ominously—a swirling barrier perpetually shadowed in eerie shades of gray, shot through occasionally with mysterious flickers of light.

Cushing Cottage, once a military stronghold, retained its austere exterior with robust observation towers and a spacious central courtyard now softened by flourishing gardens, statues, and a grand fountain. Ella peered down into the courtyard and spotted a woman in a dirtied apron collecting herbs, softly humming a hymn. Ella waved down cheerfully, but the woman merely scowled, emitted a disdainful "hmph!", and strode away.

Ella shook her head slightly, returning her gaze to the valley. Her reverie was violently shattered by the harsh clang of the iron gates. Alarmed cries rose sharply from below. She swiftly moved across the roof to investigate, observing about twenty soldiers surging into the courtyard. They wore armor or battle uniforms, armed with swords and bucklers displaying Yorke heraldry.

Ella squinted sharply for details, but her vision suddenly blurred and brightened in rapid, disorienting pulses. She rubbed her eyes vigorously, a flash of concern tightening her chest. Was this exhaustion, illness—or something more insidious? The sensations eased after a moment, but her anxiety lingered.

Refocusing, she noted the soldiers' refined uniforms and muted shoulder piping, indicative of a protective detail rather than typical guards. Highly trained and potentially deadly.

A familiar adrenaline surged through her veins. She relished this sensation, signaling adventure and purpose. But with her usual rooftop routes blocked, she swiftly descended the exterior wall to a third-floor dormer, retrieving lock picks from her utility belt. As she was working the latch, a gruff voice from below shouted, "You there!"

Ella tensed and looked down. But the voice was not directed at her. She hadn't been spotted.

The latch gave way, and she slipped quickly into the darkened interior, unseen. Voices below barked urgent orders, heightening the stakes.

Ella navigated through the dimly lit room filled with luxurious furnishings—ostentatious pieces she privately loathed. Gas lanterns flickered along the hallway, casting wavering shadows across gilded frames, thick carpets, and overly ornate tapestries.

Sudden footsteps prompted Ella to duck silently into a tiled bathroom. Holding her breath, she watched through the cracked door as a soldier walked into the empty room she'd just exited. Seizing her chance, she moved silently behind him and put a dagger to his neck before he could react.

"Quiet," she whispered fiercely. "Or I'll open your throat."

The soldier dropped his sword obediently.

"Why are you here?" she demanded softly.

"Colonel Mosley's orders," he stammered nervously. "Looking for an old lady—the Countess."

Her indignation tightened her grip momentarily. "Where's your commander? Who's in charge here?"

"Kitchen. Lieutenant Anson. Probably reading his stupid map."

Ella swiftly knocked him unconscious, hiding him and his sword beneath a nearby bed. As she moved toward the kitchen, another guard blocked her staircase descent. Ella hesitated—but suddenly, he collapsed silently. Her confusion intensified as Mrs. Baybridge stepped calmly forward, tucking a blackjack into her apron.

Baybridge's hands flashed in practiced Intel signals: "Three more ahead. I'll handle them." Then she vanished into the shadows, dragging the unconscious soldier with her.

Ella grinned widely, impressed and delighted, and carefully avoided the remaining guards.

In the kitchen, Lieutenant Anson studied a map by candlelight. Ella crept up silently and pressed her dagger firmly to his throat.

"What are you doing in my house?" she demanded sharply.

Anson stiffened, but relaxed his tone quickly. "Commander Wellington, I presume. You say it's your house, but your staff says you don't even sleep here. Quite the statement."

"I'm adjusting poorly," she admitted reluctantly, tightening her grip. "Now explain."

"I'm here by order of Colonel Cole Mosley. We must bring you to him immediately."

Two more soldiers entered cautiously, stopping short at Ella's threat. They lowered their weapons at Anson's gesture.

"Yes, Countess," Anson continued smoothly, "we mean no harm—
"

Both soldiers collapsed abruptly. Mrs. Baybridge stepped into the candlelight, a serene smile on her face.

"—Could you...ask your housekeeper to stop knocking out my men?" Anson pleaded.

"Thank you, Mrs. Baybridge," Ella said warmly. "That will be all."

"My pleasure, Countess," Baybridge replied, withdrawing elegantly.

Ella released Anson, sheathing her dagger. She noted Anson's uniform—subtle, functional, and well-crafted. She towered over him slightly, though his presence was composed.

"You haven't lost your edge," Anson remarked respectfully. "That's good. As I said, we've been urgently recalled from the front to get you. Mosley can explain further."

"I don't know this...Colonel Mosley," said Countess. "Why should I go see him?"

Anson looked uncomfortable. "Look, I wasn't supposed to say this, but Mosley's orders come from..." His voice dropped to a whisper. "Baron Greystone."

Countess's eyes widened. The Baron was her old boss in the Intelligence Corps. The big boss. Baron Greystone ran the Intelligence service for the entire kingdom, and he reported directly to King Leopold.

Ella sighed deeply, acknowledging her inevitable involvement. "Fine," she conceded firmly. "Take me to Mosley."

2

Umbra Priestess Vilma had been meditating for hours, but today, she was forsaken by Sky Mother. She tried again. Eyes closed, head bowed, and humming to herself, Vilma entered her most receptive state. But it didn't help. Sky Mother was silent.

In front of her, the portal was enormous and partially buried in the cave wall. It was Sky Mother's gift to the world: a beautiful, circular structure made of intricate, fractal patterns. The portal was the color of bone, but it had a glossy sheen that reflected light in wavy, rainbow patterns—like oil on the surface of water.

Sky Mother's Cave was a large open cavity with stalactites and stalagmites around its periphery. A small natural stream on one side brought fresh water and oxygen in. It also carried excess carbon dioxide out, so the cave could safely support large groups of pilgrims for long periods. Candles and torches lit the space, adding ambiance to its mystical air.

Surrounding the portal, and carved directly into the cave rock, were detailed statues of Sky Mother. Also, three children or assistants were often represented as helping her or worshiping at her feet. Umbra scholars were divided on their real relationship to Sky Mother. They were carved by many generations of the chosen. Some were so old that their features were almost faded smooth.

On rare, good days, Sky Mother's image and voice emerged in

Vilma's mind, a strong, otherworldly presence unlike any she had ever encountered. Sky Mother did not appear to the physical senses but rather manifested in the mind of the chosen.

Each visit from Sky Mother left Vilma awestruck, her heart swelling with gratitude. Often, Sky Mother would make strange statements that Vilma didn't understand. She said odd-sounding names of people, places, and things. Sometimes Sky Mother would list what she was grateful for. Vilma didn't understand why she did this. But sometimes, and this was most important, Sky Mother would ask for help. The first time Vilma heard Sky Mother's plea, she dedicated her life to the cause. The request was always the same. Vilma had heard it so many times that she had dedicated it to memory. Many of the chosen had. It was considered Sky Mother's most sacred message and therefore forbidden from being written down or discussed with anyone who was not chosen.

Vilma raised her head, opened her eyes, and bowed deeply to the portal, her cheek resting on her hands. Then she stood, took two steps to the side, and bent down to pick up her meditation rug.

The rug was hand-woven and exquisitely beautiful. Its corners were an array of vibrant colors and intricate patterns that mimicked the ones on the portal. In the center was the face of a young woman. She had light skin and dark hair done up in a bun. On her forehead was a tiara with three shining jewels of green, red, and blue. The woman's dark eyes were bright and confident, and she was surrounded by a halo of golden light. This was the image of Sky Mother that Vilma saw when she meditated. The loom master had faithfully reproduced it based on her description, and it was one of Vilma's most prized possessions. She carefully rolled the mat and slid it into a long, thin wicker tube, which she then slung over her shoulder.

Vilma lowered the hood of her robe and turned to leave. Her dark skin gleamed with a subtle, golden sheen in the torchlight, highlighting her high cheekbones and full lips. Her eyes, sharp and penetrating, glinted with fierce determination. Her intricately styled black hair was adorned with small pagan charms and metallic accents, adding to her regal, warrior-like presence.

Each charm and accessory in her hair was unique, many of them hand-made gifts from admirers and followers. She wore delicate, dangling earrings that shimmered with each movement, enhancing her mystical allure. Her attire, though simple in design, was accentuated by these intricate ornaments, reflecting her esteemed position within the tribe.

Vilma's body was a marvel. Her muscles were well-defined but not overly bulky. There was a grace and precision to her movements, as if every step was calculated. Her strength and poise seemed almost superhuman.

A young male attendant gasped when he noticed her. He bowed, then stared at her with excited anticipation. Vilma shook her head and looked away, ashamed. Both were disappointed.

Vilma walked out of the holy sanctum and across the outer chamber. Five attendants were chatting with each other just outside the entrance to Pilgrim's Coil. A steady flow of people was emerging from its dark recesses.

The attendants bowed to Vilma as she stepped up into the passage. Vilma would often return a smile or bow back, but now she felt dejected. Sky Mother rarely spoke, even to the chosen like her. Vilma clenched her fists, nails digging into her palms as the fury rose unbidden, a tempest of frustration and hurt. This was an important day, and Vilma felt like she deserved some support. Her tribe was going to hate her for what she was about to do, and she resented that, too. The pain made Vilma's mind seek refuge in her earliest memories: wandering Blackwater Bog, killing and eating raw food with her bare hands, going hungry for days afterward because she was so disgusted and ashamed, stealing scraps of food from anyone who had them, and finally, being taken in by the Umbra, who had given her a full belly and a warm bed after so much suffering.

***

The journey through Pilgrim's Coil usually took twenty minutes, but today the path was crowded. Several people brushed against Vilma, sending jolts of irritation through her. She fought the urge to shove them back, her hands itching to strike. Vilma found the air stifling and removed her robe, tucking it under one arm.

Her special status as Priestess afforded her some separation, but not much. Most pilgrims bowed slightly and stepped aside, but as time went on, Vilma felt more annoyed and claustrophobic. This could be her last time in Sky Mother's Cave, and she already felt the memory being fouled.

According to Umbra scripture, Sky Mother had descended into this cave, making it holy. The Coil, created by her stone helpers, was smooth and without cracks, reflecting light like glass. Attendants kept candles fresh in ornate sconces, each designed to honor Sky Mother. Pilgrims often counted each one as a meditation, but Vilma was too preoccupied with her mission.

Emerging from the Coil, Vilma took a deep breath as she entered Sky Mother's Temple. She was seething with anger but kept her composure. The temple's reverent atmosphere and awe-inspiring sights somewhat cooled her inner fire.

***

Sky Mother's Temple was a large stone building with a circular floor plan. Like Sky Mother's Cave, the temple interior was also lit by a multitude of candles. Its walls and columns were completely covered by iconic wildlife images, many faded and lost to time. Wolf, turtle, and turkey motifs commemorated the tribes who settled this region long ago. Umbra scholars called them fancy names like Munsee or Lenni Lenape, but Vilma just called them The Original People. In the center of the room, and one hundred feet high, was a magnificent stone statue of Sky Mother. She was a young woman standing on top of a round dais, her arms stretched skyward. This was the inspiration for the candle sconces. On the dais were elaborate stone carvings, separated into small, rectangular sections. Each rectangle told a story of how Sky Mother helped The Original People; from growing crops, to fishing, to building homes and shared civic spaces.

Vilma took a moment to clear her thoughts. She looked around, admiring the majesty of the temple. When she felt her calm returning, she walked outside into the cool morning air. Sobun was there, waiting for her. He was not a pilgrim and therefore not allowed inside.

Sobun was a wall of a man. At six foot two inches and two hundred and fifty pounds, his presence intimidated most people. Vilma liked it this way because it was deterrence. He wore a special camouflage uniform and had several curved, bladed weapons in sheaths across his back and on his belt. He was a Wood Shadow, one of the tribe's elite warriors, and he was her personal bodyguard.

Vilma saw a flicker of a smile when Sobun saw her, and perhaps something more, but his training and bearing came down on top of it with the weight of a forger's anvil. She also had feelings for him, if she was honest, but there was no room for desire in their relationship. Vilma had important plans, and romantic relationships were a liability she couldn't afford.

Sobun did not bow when she approached him. He was one of the few who did not have to perform the courtesy.

"Did you commune with her, Priestess?" he said. His voice seemed even deeper and more menacing than normal.

"If Sky Mother spoke, I did not hear it."

"A bad omen, I think."

"It means nothing." Vilma took the rolled mat off her shoulder and handed it to the warrior. She was suddenly filled with a longing to say something kinder to him, letting him know how she really felt. But she resisted the urge, and instead, she said, "Get Ansel and prepare to leave."

Sobun looked at her with concern, then departed. Vilma almost stopped him. She realized how mean she just sounded and regretted it. But Sobun's giant strides had already taken him out of sight, so Vilma just sighed, shook her head, and started walking toward Great Temple.

    ***

The Amenigoth temple complex was over ten thousand years old, dating back to the end of the last ice age. The smaller temples were laid out in a circular pattern around a main temple at its center. Great Temple was a massive, multi-level structure with lots of columns and vertical openings to let light in. The circular platform on which it sat was a vast green space with many lovingly tended gardens.

Vilma walked up the long and wide main steps of Great Temple toward its entrance. Four Wood Shadow guards bowed and stared as she passed. Temple guards were Wood Shadows with even more exceptional training. They had permission to savage anyone who displayed aberrant behavior, up to and including religious leaders like her.

Inside, twelve Wood Shadows were stationed at various posts around the rotunda. Several more patrolled across the open space. Vilma marched straight through the rotunda and toward two immense doors which marked the entrance to the inner chamber. A priestess with an elaborately appointed gown was there waiting.

"Bellaria," said Vilma, bowing.

The woman bowed in return. "Priestess. They are expecting you."

Vilma started walking to the immense doorway.

"Wait," said Bellaria. "I am to remind you of the protocol."

"I know the damned protocol," said Vilma. "I've been here many—

"

"And I know you know the protocol," said Bellaria. "Nevertheless, two people were beaten and dragged out of here today for disrespect."

Vilma chuckled. "Idiots."

Bellaria raised her eyebrows. "Indeed. So I tell you this, not because you do not know it, but because I have been ordered to do so. Therefore, you will conduct yourself thusly: Walk to the middle of the room and kneel on the marked spot. You will then bow low to the honored ones. You shall not speak until addressed by them. Understood?"

Vilma rolled her eyes. "Yes. Understood." She was both amused and annoyed.

"Very well," said Bellaria. She held a hand out with practiced grace, indicating the entrance to the inner sanctum. The guards on either side of the doorway stepped in and pushed the great doors inward. Vilma took her cue and walked inside.

Vilma had been inside the Great Temple inner sanctum many times, but she was always overwhelmed by it. It was a vast circular space with a very high ceiling. The floor was flat stone, adorned with a texture of thin, concentric circles. Here and there, thin columns of stone seemed to grow out of the floor, and were intricately carved to look like tree trunks. Each stone trunk was capped with a cylinder that had holes bored into it. Real but bare tree branches were inserted into the holes, and they radiated outward from each trunk, giving the illusion of an interlocking canopy overhead.

Light filtered down from the ceiling through an elaborate mesh of artificial cloth leaves and branches. The mesh projected shadows on the floor of the inner sanctum, which mimicked dappled forest light. During the day, the space was lit by natural light from outside. At night, torch sconces were slid up the walls in vertical tracks, giving the sanctum a warm orange glow.

At the far end of the chamber, a small mountain of jagged, natural stone rose out of the ground. The side facing Vilma was carved out into an almost smooth semi-circle, and into that were carved five ornate thrones. The central throne was the largest and most impressive. The two next to it were smaller and less extravagant, and the outer ones were smallest and least impressive. On each throne sat a high priest with elegant, formal robes. Three were women and two were men. The configuration changed over time, as roles changed and people's lives, deaths, or the needs of the tribe dictated. By custom, the outermost chairs were young people; twenty to thirty years old. The middle chairs were for the middle-aged, and the inner chair, the Grand Priest and head of the tribe, was an elder.

Vilma performed the ritual of kneeling and bowing, as directed. She waited patiently, but it seemed that the priests took much longer than normal to address her. Her face was getting cold and started to hurt.

"Your coming was foretold to us," said one of the younger females.

"I hope so," said Vilma, trying not to sound too sarcastic. "I made an appointment."

"No, we—"

"We know you're planning to leave," said another priest. A male this time.

"I'm…not surprised. I know you have—" Vilma wanted to say "spies", but held her tongue. "—people who report such things to you. Yes, I'm leaving. Do you want to know why?"

"Why don't you tell us?" It was the Grand Priest, his voice high-pitched, but wise sounding.

"I seek a weapon to aid Sky Mother." Vilma almost blurted it.

"And you feel it's your responsibility to gather weapons for Sky

Mother?" he said.

"The weapon is only part of its capabilities," she said, "and I have it on good authority that…"

"The arrogance," said one of the middle-aged woman.

"And what weapon is this, that you would leave our tribe to find?" said another.

"Callifrey. The rings of Callifrey," said Vilma.

There was a gasp from several of the high priests.

"A story told to excite young children," said the Grand Priest. "Nothing more."

Priestess looked from face to face, grinding her teeth as the fury rose inside her. But she said nothing.

"If you leave without permission," said one of the male priests, "you leave for good."

"The tribal rules are very clear on this," said another.

"You think this is a fool's errand," said Priestess. "A child's fairytale. I don't see it that way. This will give aid to Sky Mother—"

"Others have tried to obtain it. Many others. None returned," said the Grand Priest. "And even if you get it, there's no guarantee it will work, or even do what you think it will. Most of the scripture on Callifrey is allegory, not truth. Are they a weapon of mass destruction, as some say? A tool to control the minds of the masses? Nobody knows. It would be unwise to bet your life on such uncertainty."

The Great Priest's demeanor changed. He smiled at Priestess. "Don't go. You've been with us for so long. You are a loved and respected Umbra leader! Plus, it's dangerous out there. "

"I am strong," said Priestess. "And I have powerful friends."

"Without a doubt. But there are things beyond these walls…"

"You forget that I lived in Blackwater Bog by myself, even as a child!"

"Yes, I remember. You were a filthy little swamp rat. Stealing food from us for months before you were caught. Skin and bones! And you were so malnourished, you would have died if we hadn't taken you in when we did."

Priestess looked away. She felt herself blushing, and she balled her fists. "Our new ally will make a decisive difference."

"That abomination is not our ally, and I will caution you against taking its council."

"That abomination, as you call it, saved my life. And I'll respectfully remind you that they provided our tribe with a decade's worth of food and medical supplies!"

A female priest interjected. "Your fascination with ancient technology will get you killed. And if you bring Callifrey here, it could kill us too."

Priestess was about to lose her temper. She spoke though clenched teeth. "When I return, with the blessing of Sky Mother, I will accept your apology." She didn't wait to be dismissed. Priestess stood up, turned and started walking out of the chamber. One of the guards moved to intercept her, but saw death in her eyes. He thought better of it, and backed down.

Vilma stormed out of the council chamber, her mind a whirl of conflicting emotions. She paused in the courtyard, taking a moment to steady her breath and gather her thoughts. The high priests' dismissal of her quest had cut deep, but beneath her anger lay a steely resolve. She knew the risks, and doing nothing was not an option. Failure meant not only her own downfall but the potential loss of hope for the tribe.

She clenched her fists, feeling the weight of her mission settle heavily on her shoulders. The uncertainty was terrifying, but the potential rewards were extraordinary. Vilma's loyalty to Sky Mother burned fiercely within her, a guiding flame in the darkness of doubt. Sky Mother's voice was silent today, but Vilma felt her presence more strongly than ever. This mission was her destiny, and she would see it through, no matter the cost.

Priestess left the temple complex and gathered her small team. An hour later, they exited Amenigoth's perimeter gate, never to return.

3

Countess Ella Wellington stepped down from the armored prison carriage into the choking smoke of a smoldering world.

The ground beneath her boots was uneven and soft with blood, ash, and churned earth. The air reeked of burning pitch, scorched flesh, and the sharp tang of ozone. To her left, a man lay convulsing in his final throes of life. To her right, the twisted remains of a charred ballista wheel. Half a dozen corpses—soldiers, perhaps—were heaped together, indistinguishable save for the glint of chainmail and damaged leather.

She narrowed her eyes, taking in the hellscape of the front—less a battlefield, more a graveyard that hadn't realized it yet.

Then came the explosion.

A field cannon nearby roared unnaturally loud, followed by a crack! like the sky splitting open. The barrel burst, showering hot iron and bone fragments. One man was instantly eviscerated, another thrown back into a pile of broken siege parts. Countess calmly stepped behind the carriage as a flaming wheel bounced past her and rolled to a slow, steaming stop.

"Nice welcome," she muttered.

The command tent was no better.

It sagged under its own weight, patched and re-patched, and buzzed with the faint whine of an overworked generator. Inside, a single electric bulb flickered like a dying star above a scarred, makeshift table strewn with maps, ration tins, and half a disassembled musket.

Colonel Cole Mosley didn't bother looking up.

"You're late," he said.

His towering frame unfolded from the bench like a tired bear. His uniform was muddy, sleeves rolled up, shirt open at the collar. His face was carved from stone—bearded, weary, and unimpressed.

"Am I?" Countess asked, brushing soot from her shoulder. "I thought I arrived just in time to be almost blown to bits. I think that counts for something."

Mosley grunted. "They told me you'd be difficult."

"They told me you'd be taller."

He didn't smile. He just turned, pulled a sealed document from his breast pocket, and slapped it onto the table.

"Orders. Straight from the War Ministry. You're to proceed to Greystone Barony."

Countess didn't move.

"Baron Greystone requested you personally," Mosley added. "You don't get to say no."

"I've said no to worse men than him."

"You say no now, and I've got orders to put you on the next transport to Ravencleft. With some iron bracelets to go with your fancy royal title."

Countess crossed her arms. "What's so important in Greystone?"

Mosley's jaw tensed.

"Need-to-know. Got any more stupid questions?"

They locked eyes for a moment. Countess wasn't afraid of him—not his height, not his bulk, not even the reputation. But she could smell something in his tone: not fear, not duty. Desperation.

"Fine," she said. "But I'm not doing this because The Baron asked nicely."

"I don't think anyone expects you to do anything nicely."

He turned away and began reorganizing a stack of dispatches. Countess started for the exit.

"Oh, and Countess?"

She stopped in the doorway, glancing back over her shoulder.

"You'll have some company on the ride north."

Her brow furrowed.

"What kind of company?"

Mosley didn't answer. He was already back to muttering over a stack of maps.

Back at the carriage, the side door was open. The steam carriage hissed quietly, its pistons ticking down like a simmering kettle. She stepped up into the dim interior and froze.

There, shackled to the bench opposite her, was a man.

His clothes were bloodied and torn, his wrists bound in irons, and a filthy gag stretched across his mouth. Despite the bruises, his golden eyes burned with intelligence—and contempt.

Countess sat down across from him, arms folded, and let the silence stretch for just long enough to make a point.

Then the carriage lurched into motion, the doors slammed shut, and they were on their way.

4

Countess Ella Wellington rode in the armored prison carriage and tried not to think about the fact that she was trapped. The floor-shackled man across from her stared with intense, golden eyes. The last thing Ella was told before the carriage departed was to not interact with the man. Nor was she, under any circumstances, to remove his bonds.

"You've had better days," said Countess.

He nodded once and tilted his head, giving her a look that seemed to say, "So have you."

The sounds from the front diminished, and light from outside receded, leaving them riding in the dark. A strange feeling of emancipation washed over her. It was a kind of giddy relief that she felt in the pit of her stomach. She had to admit that she wouldn't miss the place.

Ella looked outside and saw a glint of something in the distance. As they drew closer, the carriage's external lanterns revealed a rusty, old sign in the woods. It was a white shield on a black background. In the center of the shield was: 9W. And on top, in a smaller rectangle, was the word NORTH. Countess had no idea what it meant. Was it a location? Whatever it represented, it was one of the many artifacts of the old world. A world that seeped into the present here and there, if one took the time to notice. It always impressed her, things like the sign. Despite their age, they seemed to have some kind of magical longevity.

They rode in silence for some time. Then, without warning, the inside of the carriage illuminated. Countess looked at the recessed electric bulbs overhead. She hadn't noticed they were there until they were lit. Quite nice, she thought, for a prisoner transport. Electric lights were a new phenomenon, often reserved for the wealthy. But the military was also replacing their gaslights with them.

Countess noticed a rolled paper on the seat next to her. It had the Yorke kingdom heraldry on its cover. She unfurled it and began to read. The front page covered the war with Saug kingdom. Pretty standard— it started two decades ago, and it wasn't going to end anytime soon. Blah, blah, blah. There were advertisements for several local merchants. She did her best to ignore them. Inside, there was a depressing article about how crops continued to fail. Great, she thought. Now I know why I don't read the paper.

Voices outside the carriage distracted Countess. She put the paper down and looked out of the vertical bars at a bleak scene. They were traveling through the outskirts of a town. Pirates, bandits, and people down on their luck occupied every available space. Some of their camps were out in open fields, others were in the jagged ruins of old-world buildings. Pools of orange firelight dotted the landscape. Shifty eyes and scarred, unshaven faces moved between the shadows. Their owners went about shady business, with the occasional laugh or murmur.

Someone threw a rock, which hit the side of the carriage with a loud bang. None of the soldiers outside said anything or made any move to intercept the one who had thrown it. Besides the sounds of the carriage, it was silent. Countess's senses heightened. She sat back from the window and listened for several minutes. The tension dissipated, and Countess went back to watching the world outside.

Carts, crates, and piles of sacked goods filled the gaps between the islands of light. Glints of moonlight from metal and glass revealed long-abandoned machines. Most were overgrown with a variety of plants, reclaimed by nature. Others were only elaborate homes for spiders.

The din of sound outside increased as they entered the village. It was a typical town of poor people. Everything was lit with torches or candles. Several armored town guards were standing nearby, facing south toward the bandit camps. One of them noticed her face in the window and nodded. She hid, shrinking back from the window.

The smells of cooking food reached Countess, and her stomach started to rumble. They passed an inn, which was busy. People moved about in colorful, but plain and functional clothing. None wore jewelry or carried visible coin purses. Their faces had a somber look, like they had been victims of the nearby cutthroats. It was obvious they didn't want to appear easy prey.

At the center of town, there were several partially-built structures and more people. Sounds of inebriated singing and laughing burst from a tavern. A vague smell of ale and vomit accompanied it. Several people passed by on foot, as well as another steam-powered carriage. The carriage was laden with hay, and its driver was quite drunk. The driver of Countess' carriage tooted the steam whistle twice.

A band of minstrels began to play inside the tavern. The song sounded very familiar to Countess. She was quite sure she'd heard it played at a recent awards ceremony. It could even have been at her own retirement. She wasn't sure. Sometimes minstrels tried new songs at official functions. If the song was well received there, they would move it along to a new location. This one is pleasant enough, Countess thought. And the tavern customers seemed to like it, too. They began stomping their feet in time.

Knights with and without armor sparred with various weapons in crudely-built, fenced circles. No doubt, they were preparing for the upcoming Yorke kingdom games. Representatives from several special military units would choose candidates from the winners. That is, if any survived. Other men and women outside the fences cheered the knights on. Some made bets on the outcomes of the fights. Several people had passed out on the grass from too much drink. Another intoxicated man was yelling something incomprehensible while he hugged a fence post.

A small group of children played nearby. But their idea of play was terrorizing a cat in a cage. Countess yelled at the kids, and they ran off. A little red-headed boy, who had been standing by himself, ran to the cage and freed the cat. The poor thing shot out like a crossbow bolt and disappeared behind some nearby barrels. The boy smiled, proud of himself, but made no effort to chase after the cat.

They came to the outskirts of town and its sounds receded. The carriage entered a wooded area and started up an incline. Countess heard accumulators straining, and the driver released more pressure into the system. The light from the village faded. Except for the vertical lines of an occasional tree trunk, the world outside was black.

Countess sat back and rested her eyes for a while. She felt the carriage make several lazy turns and go over several small hills. When she looked outside again, they were emerging from the woods into a large, open field. The moon was quite full, and Countess enjoyed the view. The black outline of pine trees stood out against a lighter sky.

Then, at the tree-line below, there was movement. It was a brief blur in the darkness. The shape, whatever it was, joined several more and rushed in their direction.

Outside, Countess heard several men yell. They had seen it too. Now, they readied their weapons and moved to face in the direction of the threat.

"Moob?" said the shackled man through his cloth gag.

"There's something out there," said Countess. She squinted at the black shapes. "Something moving at the tree-line. Animals maybe. I'm not sure. There's quite a few. Moving fast. Shit! They're coming right at us!"

More confused shouting outside from Mosley's men. The mass of black shapes dashed toward the carriage. Countess's first instinct was to duck and hide, but she was too horrified to look away.

Back at the tree-line, there was a rumbling in the trees. Two trunks snapped in half and fell into the field. An enormous black shape seemed to roll out of the woods, then launched itself in their direction.

Countess shook her head. Her night vision was better than most people's, but she was having trouble trying to resolve what was out there. The light of the moon was playing tricks on her.

"Dear god! What is...BRACE YOURSELF!"

There was a low, rumbling sound. It was soft at first, then grew louder. Countess felt it more than heard it. The mass of black shapes was at the carriage. WOOSH! WOOSH! WOOSH! Black shadows flew over the carriage one after the other. There were dozens of them. But they had no interest in the carriage. As fast as they arrived, they were gone.

Countess was on the floor with her arms covering her head. Outside several men screamed in terror, but the sound cut short.

"Moob!" said the shackled man.

"It's some kind of giant animal," She said. "I don't—" Countess didn't finish her sentence. Her head bounced off the carriage door, and she lost consciousness.

Something hit the carriage so hard, two of its wheels came off. It traced a lazy arc across the night sky, then landed on its side twenty feet from where it had been a few seconds ago. Lucky for its passengers, the carriage landed on the edge of a swampy area, where the ground there was soft and wet.

Countess's ears were ringing, and she couldn't catch her breath. She opened her eyes, and she was face-to-face with the shackled man. She had landed on top of him. The beautiful and terrible golden eyes glared at her in the dim light.

Something pushed the carriage down, something with massive weight. A large torrent of mud squeezed into the carriage from underneath. The carriage door, now underneath Countess, groaned under the pressure.

"Oh come on!" said Countess. Her clothes were getting fouled from the rising mud.

There was a bone-chilling sound overhead. It was a kind of low growl, something that sounded like rocks smashed together in someone's hands.

GRRRR...WHOOOSH. CLACK, CLACK, CLACK.

Countess looked up. A shadow passed overhead, then was gone. The shadow returned, then the carriage door disappeared, ripped off its hinges. Countess stared in horror at the darkness overhead. She stifled a scream when a large, glowing red eye appeared. The eye looked at her for several seconds. Then, its gaze darted around the cabin, finally settling on her fellow passenger. Countess wanted to look away, but found she couldn't. The eye blinked twice, then it was gone.

An enormous black nose forced its way into the carriage. It sniffed and readjusted itself several times, then exhaled with great force. A torrent of hot, wet snot covered Countess's head and shoulders. Too stunned to move or say anything, Countess stared up at the thing.

The nose retracted from the doorway, and the carriage seemed to rise a bit out of the mud.

Outside she heard sounds again.

GRRRR…WHOOOSH. CLACK, CLACK, CLACK. WHOOSH. WHOOSH. CLACK, CLACK, CLACK. The sounds receded. Then, they were joined by the sound of breaking branches. Then, silence.

A few moments later there were thumps on the side of the carriage. A bright orange light shone in through the top, where the door used to be.

"Anyone alive in there?" said a man's voice. It was Mosley. "Please tell me you're okay. Greystone will have my butt in a sling if…"

Countess wiped snot off her face with both hands, then slung it to the ground.

"Terrific!" said Countess, with wide eyes and bared teeth.

"Hmpf Hmpf Hmpf! Hmpf!" The shackled man was laughing his ass off.

"Shut up, you!" she said.

It took more than an hour to get the carriage off its side and its wheels reattached. This was due to the sucking mud it was submerged in. Parts of the carriage the monster had touched had an odor so foul that Mosley's men refused to go near them. It would need to be fully washed later. It wasn't long before the carriage was back in working order, and they were once again heading toward Greystone Barony.

Countess used the time to clean herself and check on the shackled man. He was fine; not much more dirty or injured than he'd started. Countess couldn't help but feel a bit resentful of that.

The moon was almost overhead. Frustrated at the silence, Ella reached over and removed the man's gag.

"So," she said, "what's your story?"

"Assassin. Intel corps," said the man. "Like you, I'm guessing."

"I'm not an assassin," said Countess. "And how do you know?"

"Way you carry yourself, I guess," he said. "And the thousand-yard-stare. Standard issue in the Intelligence corps."

Countess was impressed. Assassins weren't thugs, but they weren't usually the smartest people in the room, either.

"Not an assassin…" said the man. He raised an eyebrow. "And not an ambassador...no...not with that mouth."

"Up yours," said Countess, reinforcing the point. She was more amused than upset. "What's your name?"

"Lin. Lin Hurst."

Countess didn't know the guy. She'd never seen him before. And despite him being a fellow intel operator, she didn't trust him.

"Countess," she said.

"Ah," He said, "royalty eh? Retirement? Recent retirement, based on your age, I'd wager."

Countess nodded.

"Nice, I guess..." said Lin. "Congrats. But I ain't going out like that."

"Suit yourself," said Countess. "Why are you so roughed-up?"

"Mosley's men came for me too. Let's just say...I didn't go quietly."

"Kill anyone?"

"I have no love for these fancy, overpaid guards." He threw his head sideways, indicating Mosley's men outside. "But we're all on the same team. Fratricide ain't my thing."

A torch-lit face appeared outside the carriage window. It was one of Mosley's men.

"We approach the Barony, Countess. Bad news, I'm afraid."

Moving bits of red and yellow light played on Lin's face as he looked out the window. "Holy...oh, wow. You're not going to believe this."

Countess chuckled without mirth. "With the day I'm having, what else could go wrong?"

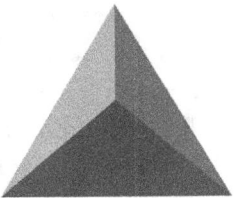

5

Greystone Barony was on fire. The broken bodies of its guards littered the ground outside the massive gate house. In the distance, across the moat, a dancing orange glow lit the barony from inside. The carriage compartment filled with the acrid smell of smoke. Countess expected screams, but all she heard was the crackle of flames and the occasional collapse of burning timber.

The carriage stopped in front of the gatehouse. Countess stepped out, her stomach immediately turning. There was a foul odor of burnt meat, wood smoke, and something worse. It was a kind of piercing, acidic smell she could not identify. She held her forearm to her face, using her sleeve as a rudimentary breathing filter. It wasn't very effective.

Lieutenant Anson was there along with ten of his men. They must have followed the carriage from the front.

Countess looked back at the carriage. The driver—and all the steam pipes and valves—blinked out of sight. She closed her eyes and shook her head. When she looked again, they were back, as if nothing had happened.

"Did you…" she said. Countess looked at Anson. There was a lot of billowing smoke, she thought. It might have blocked her view for a moment.

"What?" said Anson.

"I thought—" She looked at Anson, puzzled. "—thought I saw something weird."

"Yeah," he said. "I don't know if you've noticed, but there's a lot of something weird happening all around us."

"No. I mean—" She shot him a sour look. "Never mind."

The gatehouse doors had collapsed inward, like they were kicked in by an angry giant. The wood, a foot thick, was warped and twisted. The great hinges that once held the doors in place were pulled out of their stone moorings. The portcullis was partially melted.

Melted, Countess thought. How could it be melted? It would take the heat of a forge to do such a thing.

Countess noticed a body nearby and walked over to examine it. She could tell it was one of the Baron's personal bodyguards by the uniform. He was not wearing armor, which was normal in daily operations at the Barony. But there was something wrong with the body. The chest seemed distorted, and out of balance. It was caved-in on one side, bulged on the other, like a child might leave a molded clay figure.

Lieutenant Anson appeared next to her. "Whatever hit them, hit hard and fast. The guards didn't have time to organize a defense."

"You ever see wounds like this before?" said Countess.

"Direct hit from a ballista or catapult might do something like that."

"Maybe," said Countess. She scanned the horizon. "But If that were true, where are the projectiles? No projectiles and no siege engines anywhere nearby. Well…none outside the Barony, pointing in."

"Follow me," said Anson. "There's someone you should talk to."

Countess followed him to a wooden cart with large barrels on it. Someone had parked it next to the outer wall. Two of the lieutenant's men were standing by the cart. They were talking to a woman who sat on the ground with her back to the wall. Her eyes were wide and her dirty face was wet, like she had been crying.

"You two," said Anson. The two men turned, stood at attention, and saluted. "Go help the others secure the property. Any contact with the enemy, you fall back here. No heroics. We don't know what we're dealing with."

The two men left, and Countess kneeled in front of the woman and put her hands on top of hers. She was dressed in a dirty servant's uniform and couldn't be more than 20 years old.

"Hello miss," Countess said, putting on her most sympathetic voice. "What happened here? What did you see?"

"Pagans!" the woman said, blurting the words. "Pagans they—" She composed herself. "They had some kind of strange weapons. Like nothing I've seen before." The woman's eyes went even wider, like she was seeing the pagans in her imagination.

"Hold on, hold on," said Countess. "Slow down. You're safe now. How many were there?"

"Three," said the woman. "I saw three."

"Bullshit," said Anson. "No way three people did all this."

"I swear, sir!" said the woman. "I swear on my mother!"

Anson snorted and crossed his arms.

"You said they had...magic weapons?" said Countess. "Can you tell us more about that?"

"Two. Two had weapons. The third...he carried a small, dark box--like a case with a handle."

"What was in the box? Did he open it? Use it?" said Countess.

"No, ma'am," said the woman. "He just carried it. Must have been pretty important, too. He carried it like...like a mother carries a child."

"Tell me about the other two."

"Another man...and a woman. The box man looked small, weak. But these two were bigger. Fighters for sure." The woman looked off into space, as if trying to remember more details. "I think the woman was the leader. She yelled things to the other two. And they did what she said."

"And these magic weapons...?"

The woman squinted. "Special gloves, the woman had. Thick, like for the winter? But they had like...metal on the knuckles...here." She pointed to the back of her hand.

Anson chuckled. "So, what did these special gloves do?"

"The pagan woman hit the guards with them. But it hurt them...it hurt them bad. When they went down, they didn't get back up again."

"How so?" said Countess.

"It was like...like a rope was tied them." Said the woman. "And...and you know...the rope was pulling them really hard and fast!"

Anson furrowed his brow. "So this pagan woman. She used her

gloves to hit the guards, and they flew backward?"

"Yes! Yes, sir. They went far...backward." The woman sounded out the word. "As you say."

Countess looked at Lieutenant Anson.

"Interesting."

Anson scratched his chin. "I could use something like that at the front."

Countess ignored him.

"And the other man," she said. "What was his weapon?"

"He had like a crossbow," said the woman. "Held it to his shoulder, like this." She held her fists out in front of her face, one in front of the other.

"Ranged weapon," said Anson. "What did it shoot? Some kind of...magic arrows?" The last part he said with abundant sarcasm.

"Fire," said the woman.

"Fire?" said Countess. She pointed at one of the still burning fires.

"No." said the woman, "Not like normal fire. It was fire like...like from hell itself. Angry, red and bright! I saw black dots in my eyes for many minutes after the fire came out. And anything it shot would burn. Even stone!"

"Nonsense." said Anson. He chuckled. "We've been at war with Saug for over twenty years. I've seen some fancy weapons and equipment, but never anything like you're describing. And if the pagans have been developing weapons like this..." He paused, eying Countess. "...our intel people would have told us about them long ago."

Countess stood up. "Look around you, Anson. These are the Baron's elite guards. The toughest Yorke Kingdom soldiers. Hell, even your own men would have a hard time taking them down."

The lieutenant stared at Countess, then looked at the woman.

"Well, believe what you want," he said. "But I don't think there are any magical pagans out there."

"Something caused all this destruction," said Countess. She looked down at the frightened woman. "Personally, I take her at her word. Thank you, miss. Go home and get some rest, ok?"

"Thank you, ma'am," said the woman. She stood, swayed slightly, then walked off without looking back—still half-lost in whatever horror she'd witnessed.

"You know there are things out there," Countess said, when the woman was out of earshot. "Things from the old world. Things we're not supposed to see. You know what I mean."

"I do," said Anson. "I've turned-in my share of colorful little trinkets to our intel liaison. But nothing I would have called a weapon."

"That's not what I mean. I mean working things. Important things."

"Look, uh…" Anson looked away and started to sweat. "…we're not supposed to talk about that, and I won't discuss it now. If you're trying to trick me into--"

"No," said Countess. "Nothing like that. I just want you to admit that one could find something out there that has…let's say…novel properties."

"Novel?" said Anson. "Maybe. I don't know. But what I just heard sounds like a fairy tale. And I need more evidence than just one servant woman's word on the matter. I guess I'll concede the point. I'm a soldier, not a detective."

"Well leave the detective work to me," said Countess. Then she smiled and clapped him on the shoulder. He was startled, clearly not used to such familiar gestures while in uniform.

"But I understand where you're coming from."

Anson looked away.

"I'm going in," said Countess. "I have to find the Baron."

"Unwise," said Anson. "You should let us clear the area, first."

"No time. He could be in trouble."

"And he could be dead. Those pagans could still be in there. If you go in and get killed, that's on you. My official report will state that I warned you against such action."

"Duly noted, Lieutenant," said Countess, with a flippant salute. "But I've been sneaking around this place a couple of decades now. Got a few tricks up my sleeve."

Anson crossed his arms. "Obviously. At least take a couple of my men with you."

"They'd just slow me down," said Countess. "And they'd give away my position. Plus, you need your men to secure the Barony. Take care, Lieutenant Anson. I hope to see you on the other side."

Anson stood at attention and saluted. "Countess."

Countess turned and jogged through the ruined entrance of the gatehouse. Anson watched her go, then smiled.

"Good girl," he said. "You'll get it right this time."

6

The Outer Bailey of Greystone Barony was a vision from hell. Crops and buildings were ablaze. People ran in all directions, shouting orders, dragging buckets, trying desperately to contain the chaos.

The bodies of at least ten men were strewn about on the ground nearby. They were all barony guards. Dark tendrils of smoke curled from the seams of their plate armor. The smell was foul—part grease fire, part slow-roasted meat. Their bodies had cooked inside the steel. The blackened metal still radiated heat and a stench that turned her stomach.

The smoke was useful, though. It made good cover. Countess donned her cloak. Then, she made her way to the entrance of the inner Bailey without anyone noticing her. She stopped to look and listen. The doors to the Inner Bailey were open. The guards had no time to close them during the attack. There was no sign of activity around her, so she peeked inside.

Countess took several minutes to scan the area. Greystone Barony looked big from the outside, but inside, it was enormous. It was an amazing feat of engineering and architecture. Buildings and structures were packed in, the space optimized. But it never felt crowded.

The gardens of the inner Bailey were always beautiful and well-manicured, even in winter. It was late summer now, and everything was still in bloom. As Countess scanned the landscape, she saw vibrant blossoms in full bloom. The air was filled with the scent of roses and jasmine, and butterflies flitted from petal to petal. It was a stark contrast to the chaos outside.

Countess took a deep breath, trying to ground herself. But as she continued to observe, the flowers flickered, their colors dimming and then disappearing entirely. The once lush garden became a barren, desolate landscape, devoid of life. She blinked and rubbed her eyes, but the barren scene persisted for a moment longer before the flowers reappeared, their colors more saturated than before.

She shook her head, wondering if her mind was playing tricks on her. "Is this real?" she whispered to herself, touching a nearby rose. It felt soft and real under her fingertips, but she couldn't shake the feeling that something was off.

Her senses seemed unusually sharp today, almost too sharp. The sweet scent of the flowers returned, and the vibrant colors filled her vision once more. She hoped this wasn't a sign of fatigue or the stress of the situation getting to her.

On a typical day, Countess would take her time and admire the flowers and statuary. She would try to get lost in the myriad nooks and crannies which hid secrets and delights. There were abundant plaques, all dedicated to the heroic deeds of intelligence agents. And there were giant, complex statues dedicated to famous battles. It was enough to make even the most jaded person emotional.

Beyond the gardens, to the left was the king's residence. It was a large cottage with several support buildings for staff, when the king visited. Behind that, was a large hospital and a well-appointed pub. She spent many nights there, drinking herself into oblivion.

On the right was the chapel, amphitheater, and great hall. Each could hold hundreds of people. Behind those, the mortuary and graveyard. There were also support buildings, small farms, herb gardens, and recreational parks. The Inner Bailey was a self-sustaining town inside one wall.

Countess slunk inside. She darted across the open ground separating the inner Bailey wall from the gardens. Satisfied she wasn't detected, she moved through the gardens toward the Keep.

Greystone Barony's keep was an enormous building complex. Constructed of large, interlocking black stones, the edifice was stark and imposing. Some even found it repulsive. Others were quite sure the place was haunted. The keep was later named Intelligence Headquarters. It was one of Yorke Kingdom's first major construction projects. Hundreds of years old, it was filled to the brim with history, rare objects, and secret passages. On any given day, it was also packed with important people. And as Countess was always reminded, intelligence agents were not.

Countess zigzagged between shadows, making her way to the headquarters entrance. There were two abandoned goods carts at the right service door. The carts' spilled produce littered the ground.

Several dead guards were on the ground in front of the headquarters entrance. And the twin front doors were wide-open. There were no lights on inside. Countess was quite concerned by this. The building used both gas and electric lighting. The electric lights were new, experimental, and expensive. The gas lights were inexpensive, but more numerous. They were connected together via a complex pipe manifold. Both systems had sources deep underground. They were completely separate and had many redundancies. It would take a concerted effort by trained personnel to defeat both systems. Countess could do it, but only because she had special training.

Countess dashed up the short flight of stairs to the front doors. She stood off to the side and peeked in. No one was present, and there was no sound. She stepped in and winced when the sound of her footstep reverberated off the marble floor. Reaching into her waist pouch, she pulled out a pair of soft booties, then slipped them over her shoes. They provided a nice insulating barrier to the floor. Now she could move about with much less sound.

Countess slid her feet across the floor, like she was ice-skating. Gliding across the foyer, she built up speed. She twisted around, then slid backward, softly into the shadow of a column.

The entrance hall was a good representation of the fine decor of the building. Suits of armor, shields, ornate tapestries, and fancy oil paintings decorated the walls. Every table had a piece of the kingdom's military history on top of it. And the room was filled with helmets, fancy boxes filled with colorful medals, and weapons.

Countess took a moment to recall her years of experience in this building. She knew its secrets, the hidden doors, and the peep-holes. She had spent countless hours exploring every nook and cranny, learning its layout like the back of her hand. Her thoughts wandered to the times she had used these passages to evade detection or to gather intelligence unnoticed.

A side door opened. Two staff members, a man and a woman, entered holding lit candles in front of them.

"I think they're gone now!" whispered the man. "Don't worry. I'll protect you."

"Like you protected me when I almost fell over the railing?" Countess could tell that the woman was being silly and flirtatious.

"We were kissing at the time," said the man. Then he reached out and grabbed her around the waist. "And I did catch you before you fell."

"Clumsiest catch I've ever seen in my life," said the woman. She giggled and pushed him away.

"Hey," he said. "I think there are more candles and supplies in this cabinet."

The man walked a few steps, then stepped on something.

"Wha—" The man hunched over to look at what he was standing on. There was a loud click and whoosh. A large clump of black goo shot up onto the man's face, then exploded. The now headless body fell to its knees, then slumped over onto its side.

The woman let out an ear-piercing scream, then turned to run. She tripped over something, then fell onto the floor, silent and motionless.

Countess slid over to the woman. She saw a large arrow shaft sticking out of her head, and a pool of dark liquid expanding around her head.

"Shit," Countess said under her breath. "The bastards left traps."

Intelligence headquarters was legendary for its secret passages. Hidden doors and little peep-holes to observe people without them knowing were plentiful. For those who knew they existed, it was a constant game to find new ones. Or, to use them in creative ways to blow the minds of the uninitiated. The higher-ups discouraged their use. Some even gave out reprimands to those they caught. To their mind, these things were hidden and secret for a reason. Countess had been caught once. She was forced to write passages from the Employee Handbook over and over. She remembered it well. "Chapter 2, Employee Conduct. Clandestine infrastructure within the Intelligence Headquarters building is for official business only. It should only be used where diplomacy fails, or in dire situations, to subvert an enemy."

Countess was sure she was operating within the guidelines of official policy now. And after working in the building for twenty years, she was confident she knew most of its secrets. Countess had to get to the Baron's office, which was on the third floor. She slid over to the large entrance hall fireplace, where she removed and stored her booties. Stepping onto the hearth, she ducked her head under the lintel. A small, vertical lever was hidden there. Once actuated, a panel inside the fireplace slid aside. It revealed a metal ladder leading upward.

As the faux panel reseated itself, sealing her in darkness, Countess sighed, climbed back down, and fished the beta tube from her pouch. The light was considered a mission-critical item, and she would tend to agree. It was issued by "the techies," men in a small, creepy office beside the quartermaster. They preferred the company of cool gadgets to other human beings.

The vial glowed with a soft, greenish light—some kind of phosphorescent jelly the techies swore would last a decade. Countess didn't ask how. She'd learned not to. Ella always carried it with her. It was a constant companion for her other waist pouch necessities— things like her blade, lock picks, and compass. There were other things she always packed in her pouch, but they were less critical; like a pencil, small pad of paper, and implements to start a fire.

The beta light tube was seated inside a small, black rubber housing, allowing it to be held in the hand or mouth. She chose the latter, as her hands were going to be occupied.

***

Countess climbed the ladder and paused at the second floor. This level was administrative offices, libraries, and housekeeping. She didn't need anything here, so she kept climbing. Reaching the third floor, she found and actuated another lever. This one opened a panel into a small broom closet.

Countess dismounted the ladder, put her beta light away, and went to the door to peek out. Nothing. There was no sound and the entire area seemed abandoned.

She left the closet and moved down a hallway, staying crouched and making as little sound as possible. The hallway ended in a large open area.

Most considered the first floor to be quite well appointed. But the third floor was grandiose. This was the realm of Baron Greystone. Not quite the opulence of the royal palace at Mohonk Castle, but it was every inch, built to impress. To start, the ceilings were several feet higher than on lower levels. The effect made you feel smaller, less significant. And every wall was ornate. They were either paneled in dark wood or filled with treasures. Rare weapons or exquisite oil paintings hung from them. The paintings all featured some kind of pompous dignitary or high-ranking military officer.

The area even smelled extravagant. The scent was complex and exotic. It was part wood polishing cream and part potpourri. Bowls filled with the stuff were on every table in sight. Inside were aromatic herbs, spices, and oils gathered from the Barony gardens.

Movement ahead forced Countess to stop and take cover. It was one of the pagans. She watched him for several minutes. He was patrolling an area between two large meeting rooms. The floor on this level was covered by fancy carpet, so she didn't have to worry about anyone hearing her footsteps.

Countess hid in a nook beside a display case. The case contained older and larger versions of the tools she used to do her work. Many were impressed by them, but they didn't have to do Countess's work. If they did, they would laugh as she did when she saw them. Her predecessors were out of their minds to carry around such clumsy things!

Countess made a careful approach toward the pagan. He was scruffy, unshaven, thin, and of average height. His clothes were rags, like sewn-together burlap sacks. But to his advantage, they were a mixture of dark, matte, and natural colors. They blended in well with the environment.

In the corner of her eye, Countess saw something out of place. It was a shadow on the floor near the wall where there shouldn't be one. She moved her head around, trying to resolve some more details of the thing, but it didn't work. She had to get closer. She crept toward the thing and stopped. It was one of the pagan traps. An almost invisible strand connected it to a table leg on the other side of the room. It was a trip wire.

Countess reached into her waist pouch and pulled out a small cutting tool. It had dark-red rubber handles, and she usually used it for electrical wires. But it would do quite well for this job. She held the line firmly with one hand, then clipped the thread, slowly releasing the tension. The device made an almost imperceptible click. It was now disabled. She exhaled slowly and smiled.

Countess then turned her attention to the pagan. She waited for him to stop near the far extent of his patrol, then sneaked into the closer office. When he walked by, he was mumbling something incoherent to himself.

Dagger drawn, Countess sprang out at him, then pulled him back into the office with her. She covered his mouth with one hand, and with the other, jabbed him twice in the neck with the point of her dagger. Most civilized folks would get the idea when Countess lay the flat of her blade against their necks. Pagans always needed a little more encouragement.

"Don't make a sound," she said, "or this goes across your throat."

"Oh, uhhh--" he said. Countess cut him off with a savage squeeze.

"I said quiet!" she whispered.

"Ok! Ok!" he whispered. "What do you want?"

"Information."

"Fine!"

Countess gagged. The man smelled awful. He had a kind of fishy, rotten earth smell. It was the smell of the swamps where they lived. And beneath that, Countess noticed a sweet and sour odor. It was the berry-flavored moonshine they made (and illegally sold).

"I don't know much," he said. "We were told to meet here. Three of us. Paid a whole month's work in advance. All we have to do is secure the top floor of this building. And at dawn, we disappear."

"Who paid you?"

"Don't know."

"How can you not know who hired you?" said Countess. She was getting angry.

"We all got letters. Didn't see anyone. It was strange. We all talked about how strange it was."

"And you always do jobs for people who just send you letters?"

"Might've... left out the part where they threatened our families."

"Oh. I guess that makes sense." Countess put away her dagger and drew out her blackjack.

"I just have one more question," she said. Then she knocked him out.

Countess found another trap. It was the same type of pressure-triggered explosive that had killed the staffer. She thought of a plan for the trap. But using it would make noise, so she'd only have a short amount of time to pull the plan off. Countess found a broom and used it to slide the trap across the floor. She placed it out in front of a column where the second pagan was patrolling.

Countess hid behind the column and waited for the pagan to pass.

"Pst," said Countess.

"What the—" The man took two steps forward. Then his foot landed on the trap.

He looked down.

"Shit!"

Countess covered her ears. The explosion was loud and sounded messy. As expected, the last pagan ran in her direction. Countess moved sideways in the shadows and waited.

When the pagan ran past, she jumped on his back and clubbed him hard on the head with her blackjack. He didn't go down, but he was dazed. She got him into a chokehold and squeezed as hard as she could. He tried to slap at her, but it wasn't effective. He was down and out in less than thirty seconds. She moved back into the shadows and waited for more pagans to arrive. None did.

Countess stood, smiling, sweating, and out of breath. She felt great. Her retirement was too comfortable, and she missed this.

Countess continued toward the Baron's office. She passed the bodies of several more guards and staff and had to disarm another tripwire.

The Baron's office was actually a suite of offices and conference rooms that took up one third of the top floor. The opposite side was the Baron's domicile, and the War Room was in the middle of the two. The War Room was a large space with long tables, where people with long titles discussed large things. Countess had never been in there, and never wanted to be. She avoided the pretentious place.

Countess arrived at the door to the Baron's office. She was amused to discover that it had a fancy new plaque. It read: Baron Thaddeus Greystone, Minister, Yorke Kingdom Intelligence.

Countess smirked. "Baron Fancy Plaque," she muttered. "Of course you are."

7

The door to the Baron's office was open, and so was the entrance to his safe room. To Countess's disappointment, he was in neither.

"Shit," Countess whispered. "Where the hell are you?!"

Moonlight spilled through the Baron's tall windows, casting pale lines across the room—just enough for Countess to work. She started with his desk, rifling through the drawers. There was nothing out of the ordinary. In the waste basket, nothing interesting. Everything in his office proper was normal and orderly, so she went back into the safe room.

The Baron's safe room was a rumor and a legend. Everyone suspected he had one, of course, but it was never confirmed. No one had ever seen it, until now. Countess was surprised that it was a lot smaller and less fancy than she expected. In her imagination, it was a lavish space with a wet bar and full to the brim with treasure and secret documents. It turned out to be a small, featureless metal box, with a desk, chair, and a few unremarkable boxes. Inside the boxes, just dull stacks of official correspondence.

One thing did stand out: The Baron's humidor. It was a very fancy wooden box with intricate designs etched into it. The box seemed very old to Countess. It was heavy and seemed to be hand-carved. The designs were strange and beautiful. The sides depicted a pre-pagan society, their lives etched in miniature wilderness scenes. The most intricate design was on the top. It showed a group of these people receiving a gift from a holy woman.

The Baron always kept the humidor on his desk. What was it doing back here? This was the sign she was looking for, a detail that only she would notice.

Countess examined the outside of the humidor. Nothing added or out of place. She tried to open it, but found it locked. There was a little diamond-shaped ornament on the front of the box. Countess discovered that, if she slid the ornament to the side, it hid a keyhole.

She put the box down, drew out the lock pick set from her waist pouch, and went to work. Child's play. She had it open in seconds. Inside…cigars. No surprise there. She dumped them out.

"Sorry Baron," whispered Countess.

A small piece of white card was in there with them. She picked it up. There was writing on one side. It said: "Countess—expected you, but couldn't stay. It's not safe. Find me. Down where the dusty armored sentinel points."

"Great," whispered Countess. "A riddle?"

Ok, she thought. So…downstairs somewhere? Hmm…dusty sentinel. The basement, most likely. Why there, though? What was down there? Not much. A wine cellar, a jail, some storage rooms.

Countess had been down there a few times, looking for something interesting. She never found anything. Well, that wasn't quite true. There was one time she had some fun down there. Some idiot had gotten drunk at the pub and mistook the headquarters building for his dorm. Security found him peeing in one of the office flower pots. She had been serenaded by several of his crazy shanty songs. The more amusing part was how pissed the guard was. He took the job so he could sleep and get away from his nagging wife. That night he had to work. The guy complained to himself at length, until she departed. He wouldn't shut up!

Wait, Countess thought. There was an old suit of armor down there. Dusty? A little. Definitely covered in cobwebs. She couldn't remember it pointing at anything, though. It was the only suit of armor down there, and the only thing that could be considered an "armored sentinel." It was a good lead.

Countess left the Baron's office suite and considered her next move. She wanted to avoid the main stairs as the pagans likely set traps there. Her best bet was an alternate route, like the one she'd used to get up here. She didn't know of any secret passages on this side of the third floor, but the second floor was lousy with them. She'd have to take her chances on the top section of the main stairs.

Countess backtracked to the main stairs and looked down. Sure enough, there was something suspicious on one of the stairs, about halfway down. It was risky, but the large wooden bannister was otherwise free of obstructions.

"Well," Countess whispered. "I've always wanted to try this…"

She climbed out on the bannister and let herself slide down backward. On the way down, she had to suppress the desire to yell "Weeeeee!" At the bottom, still mounting the bannister, she examined the ground nearby. There was nothing suspicious, so she climbed down and crouched.

The nearest library, one specializing in books on weaponry, was her best bet. It was a short way down the hall. She made her way there and opened one of the double doors to peek in. It was pitch-black and quiet, so she took out her beta light and put it in her mouth. She knew this level well enough to find her way in the dark. But she was in a hurry, so the visual advantage helped.

Countess went to a corner in the far rear of the room and found the bookshelf she was looking for. Ducking down, she looked under one of the shelves and found the little red lever there. She thumbed it, waited for the bookcase to swing out of the way, then stepped into the open passage. A few moments later, the bookcase slid back into place without a sound.

The room was small and full of random junk. It had a few storage boxes, some fancy candlesticks, and a few paintings which were leaning against the wall. In the corner, there was a metal ladder. It led down, but did not extend up to the third floor. She climbed onto the ladder and started her descent.

It was a long climb down to the basement. It felt to Countess like it took twice the time to climb down than up. The ladder ended in a large, open area with a dark wooden floor. The room was another storage space. Wooden crates were stacked here and there. All were covered in cobwebs. There was not much else there.

The room smelled stale and dusty, but along with that, was a subtler scent of rotten wood and damp earth. Several windows, high up on the wall, let dim light in from ground level. Countess could see well enough, so she stored her beta light and continued to scan the room.

Something moved by one of the wooden crates. It came darting across the floor at her. Countess's hair stood on end. She grabbed for her dagger.

Oh, hell no, she thought. It was a giant spider. Its bright green body was the size of her hand! Countess instinctively kicked at it, and missed. It dodged out of the way, stopped, then hissed at her. Then, it stood up on its hind legs. She took another swipe at it. This time her foot landed with a leathery thump, and the spider flew back into the shadows.

Countess had enough time to reposition the dagger in her hand. She was now holding it by the point. The spider shot out at her, and she flung her dagger at it. It hit the spider in the head, pinning it to the floor. She jumped onto its abdomen, sending its iridescent insides splattering in all directions. Countess bent over, put her hands on her knees, and took several deep breaths.

"Oh God," she whispered. "I hate spiders."

Countess retrieved her dagger, then she did her best to clean her boots on one of the nearby crates. It was a shoddy job, but at least she got the big chunks off.

"Disgusting!"

Countess looked around the room for a way out. There were no doors. One of the walls had a red lever at eye level. She actuated it, and part of the wall slid sideways into a recess. A torch-lit hallway was on the other side.

Countess peeked out into the hall, checking both directions. It was quiet, there was no one present. She stepped out into the hallway, and the wall closed behind her.

She was near the storage rooms and very close to the suit of armor. Countess found it right where she left it: guarding an unremarkable, dead-end hallway. This was why nobody gave it a second thought. She gave it a once-over. Yep. Cobwebby-as-ever.

Countess froze in place. There were dark red patches and streaks all over the ground. Blood, and lots of it. If the person hadn't been killed outright, they were seriously wounded for sure. She hoped it wasn't the Baron, but she feared the worst.

She looked back at the armor. Where it points, she thought. It wasn't pointing anywhere, only holding its hand out. She followed where the fingers pointed. Just a wall on the opposite side. Nothing there.

As she moved closer, she noticed a figure by the armor statue. It was one of the Baron's guards. The man was examining the wall across from the statue. Something about him seemed off, and as she got closer, the smell hit her. The swampy, fishy odor unmistakably marked him as a pagan.

Countess approached cautiously. "What are you doing here?" she asked, applying her most authoritative voice.

The man jumped slightly, then turned to face her, a too-quick smile spreading across his face. "Just...checking for traps, miss. Orders from the Baron."

There was a twinkle in his eye. He was watching her closely. And his words were smooth. A bit too smooth for her liking. Countess knew a lot of the Baron's guards. They all had a certain bearing about them; mannerisms, a way of moving their bodies. This man had none of them. And the smell. The smell was a dead giveaway.

Countess tightened her grip on her dagger. "You smell like the swamp."

The man's smile faltered. "Just got back...from a mission there."

Without wasting another second, Countess lunged at him with her dagger.

He was quick! He dodged, drawing a short sword with a curved blade. His swipe caught her shoulder, slicing through her clothing and biting into her flesh. She hissed in pain but moved swiftly, dodging his second strike and retaliating with a slash of her own that left a long gash across his cheek.

The pagan grunted in pain. Countess was matching his speed. He changed tactics out of sheer frustration. He tried to overpower her with brute strength, tackling her to the floor and pinning her down. Countess struggled against the weight of him. Her arms were immobilized, but her lower body was free, so she kneed him hard in the groin.

He growled savagely and curled up in pain, giving her the moment she needed to get behind him and press her dagger to his throat. "Who are you? Who are you working for?" she demanded.

The pagan groaned, his face twisted in pain. "To hell with you, City!" He spit after he said it. At this range his odor was overpowering, and his breath was somehow twice as bad. Countess' eyes began to tear-up.

She had been around pagans long enough to know that "City" was a shortened and derogatory form of "city dweller".

"Don't test me," said Countess, her grip tightening. "I will slit your throat. Tell me. Who are you working for!"

"Ah! Ah!" he managed to say. "Priestess. Told to call her Priestess. Don't know her real name."

"Who is she?" Countess pressed, but he turned defiant, and said no more.

She knocked him out with the hilt of her dagger and quickly hog-tied him with some hide straps she kept in her pouch for the purpose. "You're lucky I don't kill unless I have to," she muttered, leaving him for the guards to find.

Countess grabbed a nearby torch from its sconce, then crossed over to take a closer look at the wall. She didn't see anything at first. Then, something caught her eye. It was a small white button in the mortar between two stones. It stood out because it was covered by a bloody fingerprint.

"Not good," said Countess under her breath. "Not good at all."

She was usually excited about discovering new secrets, but this one was dreadful. Sweating, Countess stood off to the side with her dagger drawn. She clicked the button, then tensed up, ready for anything. She was not prepared for what she saw on the other side.

Countess peeked into the opening where the stone wall slid out of sight. The room, if she could call it that, was brightly lit by flat, dull-green rectangles on the ceiling. If they were electric lights, she had never seen their like. The flat, white walls were impossibly smooth. They reflected light like dull glass, or a pond after a storm. The King's palace didn't have walls that finely crafted.

Other things tugged at her mind. There were expertly manufactured objects affixed to the walls. She could not identify any of them. And they had labels affixed to them, or beside them, that didn't make any sense. She could read them, but she could not derive their meaning.

The room, she realized, was not a room at all, but the top landing of a stairway. There were stairs leading down and around the corner. Countess was quite alarmed by everything she saw. But the worst part of this foreign place, were the long streaks of blood. Someone's body had been dragged down the stairs and out of sight.

8

Countess carefully descended the alien stairs. Fear and panic grew inside her with each step. Unfathomable shapes surrounded her, and she was having a difficult time processing them. She lacked even the vocabulary to describe what she was seeing—geometry bent wrong, materials that shimmered like frozen smoke, angles that made her stomach twist. She focused on her goal: finding the Baron and understanding what he needed from her in this strange place.

The air here assaulted Countess's sense of smell. It was oppressive—a rank cocktail of human sweat, old socks, sour rot, industrial chemicals, and something sharp and alien, like burning metal doused in sugar. Countess winced and held her nose. This assault on her senses only heightened her anxiety, but she forced herself to continue.

At the bottom of the winding stairs, there was a short corridor. It led to an open area which terminated in a vertically bisected wall. The bottom half of the wall was dominated by a pattern of diagonal black and yellow stripes. The top half was a large rectangle of opaque black glass. About halfway down the corridor, the trail of blood ended. It looked partially cleaned at the far end, the job obviously left unfinished. The sight of blood made her heart race—was the Baron in danger?

Countess felt completely exposed. There were no shadows here, no place to hide. The entire area was bright and evenly lit, like the noon sun, but there were no visible light sources. She wondered who could maintain such a place in a world so devoid of the technology she was used to. Countess entered the open area with her dagger drawn. She was expecting to get jumped at any moment.

There was a loud pop, which reverberated off the walls. Countess froze in place.

"Stop right there," said a voice. The voice was loud and had a strange metallic quality to it. It had a similar quality to one she had heard as a child. She and her friends had made paper cones and yelled at each other through them.

"You can put your weapon away," said the voice. Countess sheathed her dagger, her mind racing to understand what kind of place she had stepped into and who was commanding her.

"See that red X on the floor?"

Countess looked down. "I see it."

"Walk over to it," said the voice, "kneel down, and lace your fingers together on top of your head."

"How delightfully specific," Countess whispered to herself. She had to decide quickly if compliance was her best option. "And if I don't comply?" she said, testing her captors.

"Don't test me, Countess Wellington," said the voice. Flat. Mechanical. Without hesitation.

"You know who I am?" she said.

"We know who you are," the voice sounding tired and impatient. "Let's just get through this."

Countess walked to the red X, kneeled, then put her hands on her head. She had the urge to flee but forced herself to stay calm. Her curiosity was piqued—how did they know her? What did they want?

"Look forward," said the voice. "Do not turn your head."

Countess heard doors open on both sides of the room. Several people ran toward her. Bright red points of light appeared on the floor and seemed to dance around together.

"What--" said Countess. The sudden light show dazzled her.

"Eyes front!" said a muffled woman's voice.

"Check her," said a male voice, also muffled.

Countess felt gloved hands pat her in various places. There was heavy breathing in her ear, like someone huffing into a long wooden box. She didn't know what to make of it, feeling more like an object than a person. Her anger simmered beneath the surface.

"Aside from the dagger, she's clean," said the woman.

"Did anyone follow you in here?" said the male voice.

"No," said Countess. "I'm alone."

"Good. Now stand up, turn left and head through the door in front of you."

Countess did so. She glanced at one of the people she was being interrogated by, and immediately regretted it. They were wearing suits of complex-looking black armor. It was the craziest thing she'd ever seen. There was no metal on the suits. Matte-black laminate fabric hugged their limbs, pouches snapped to their belts and vests like modular insect segments. They all wore helmets, with dark reflective visors that hid their faces. Countess saw herself reflected in them and wondered what they saw reflected there—an intruder, a threat, or the ghost of a world long buried.

A hand grabbed her forcefully on the back of the neck and pushed her forward. Countess stumbled.

"Inside," said the female voice. "Now."

"Easy!" said Countess. She walked through the door into an even more alien world. Countess could hear the door close behind her, and the way it seated, she could tell it was formidable. There were three loud clunks as the door's locks seated themselves.

"Turn right," said the male voice. "Walk to the end of the hallway."

Countess reached the end of the hallway and looked right. She was in the area behind the large black rectangle. But from this vantage, Countess could see clearly outside to the red X where she had been kneeling. So they could see out, but she could not see in. It was an interesting magic trick, she had to admit. The reality of the room stunned her. Countess's eyes darted around the complex environment. There were little multi-colored lights everywhere. More strange objects, many of them looked like children's toys. Again, her mind strained to take it all in—like trying to read a book written in a dream.

"Sorry about the shake-down," said the male voice. Countess looked at him as he took off his helmet. "Marcus Avery," he continued. "Connector security team captain, at your service."

"Nice to meet you, Captain," said Countess, trying to regain some composure.

The man was about 25 years old, dark-skinned and clean-shaven. He had piercing eyes that she found very intimidating. But the most interesting thing about him was his hair. She had never seen hair like his before. It was like a perfect work of art. Bare skin around the ears transitioned to a rounded, skull-hugging cap at the top of his head. He noticed her staring.

"Like my hair?" he said.

"It's amazing," Countess said. "I've never seen anything like it."

"Standard military fade," he said, amused at her fascination.

"How is it cut so precisely?"

"Beats me," he said, and laughed. "I'm kidding. We have devices...little hand tools that do it. I'll show you some time."

"The pagans left explosive and chemical irritant projectile traps in the HQ," said the female team member, taking off her helmet. "We had to make sure you weren't followed or tracked anything in here with you."

Countess was at her limit. "Look, I don't understand any of this. Why did you bring me here? What is this place?"

"I know you're feeling overwhelmed," said a new voice. It was Baron Greystone. He walked into the room through an elevated door at the far end of the room, and to her surprise, he looked perfectly healthy.

Countess stood at attention and saluted. "It's good to see you, Baron Greystone. I thought you were seriously wounded...or worse."

The Baron smiled. "There's no need for that formality here. And now that you're a Countess, I consider you a peer!" The man laughed, finding that last part quite humorous.

"I'm alive and well. But you're probably referring to all the blood up at the Connector entrance."

"Yes, sir."

The Baron gestured to several vaguely human-shaped black bags on the floor nearby.

"Several of my staff were killed up there." The Baron's voice grew quiet. "Including my chief advisor, Demetrius Blackwood. A terrible loss—and a warning, I think." The Baron looked off into the distance, glassy-eyed.

"I'm sorry for your loss, sir," said Countess, genuinely saddened by the loss of life. She wondered what kind of threats they were truly facing.

"War is hell, Countess, as you well know." He looked regal in his uniform, with his hands clasped behind his back. "Welcome to The Connector. You can think of it like an underground warehouse. But this warehouse is one of many that feed into a larger warehouse nearby. It's a regional hub facility called Iroquois Warpath."

"Fancy," said Countess. "And a fancy name, too."

"Very," said the Baron. "For reference, there are enough supplies in this facility for a thousand people to live comfortably for ten years. Iroquois Warpath has a warehouse large enough to supply ten thousand people for over one hundred years. You get the idea."

Countess blinked. That was army-level quartermaster scale—beyond anything she'd seen. This place could feed a kingdom.

"I know," said the Baron. "It's a lot to take in."

"Why keep all these supplies down here?" said Countess. "What's the purpose?"

"We suspect it connects to something...much bigger. Other facilities, perhaps. Or something even stranger. But the truth is, we don't know. Something is connected to the other side which is supplying a lot of people with everything you can think of, from food to fuel to baby clothes. Hand tools to large, industrial equipment. And stuff we don't even understand—what it is or what it does. And here's another challenge, we don't have access to Iroquois Warpath. The security there is lethal. Automated defenses kill anyone who goes near it."

"Automated?" said Countess.

"You'll learn more about that later," said the Baron.

"Amazing," said Countess, "and terrifying."

"Exactly," said Baron Greystone. He looked off into the distance. "And humbling. If I could apply this level of logistics to the war effort against Saug, we'd end the conflict in a week! Unfortunately, the machinery down here is ancient. And the ability to build or repair some of it is lost to time." The Baron sighed, and looked at Countess seriously. "That's enough for now. I have some people I'd like you to meet."

The Baron turned and began walking out of the room. "Please

come with me."

Countess climbed the short flight of stairs and followed the Baron through the door. He started down a long, wide, and brightly-lit hallway with many doors along its length. As they walked, Countess noticed several framed photographs on the wall to her left. They were all faded images of previous Connector facility commanders. The first two were United States Air Force Generals. The third was from an organization called Phoenix.

Timothy Horton, Brigadier General, Air Force Logistics Command
Peter Amon, General, Air Force Materiel Command

The third, a less faded photo, showed a man in a fancy suit with a Phoenix logo pin on the lapel. The caption read: "Mr. David Chase, Associate Vice President, Phoenix Logistics Division"

The names meant nothing to her. But the title "Air Force" and the clean-cut suits hinted at a civilization with power far beyond her own.

"What does…Material Safety Data Sheet mean?" asked Countess carefully. "And…halon fire extinguisher? I mean, I think I understand from the context that you use it to put out a fire, but what is halon, please?"

The Baron stopped and stared at her for a moment, then sighed. "I know you have questions, Countess. But now is not the time to answer them. We have to focus on the current threat."

"The pagans," said Countess.

"Precisely."

"I've seen evidence that the main pagan leadership may have already left the Barony," said Countess.

"Yes," said the Baron. "They departed hours ago. Just before you arrived."

"Wait," said Countess. "How do you know when I arrived?"

"Not important."

"But—"

Baron Greystone stopped at a doorway to their right, stared at Countess for a moment, then entered the room.

"Come in and close the door." He looked behind her and said, "You two. Make sure we're not disturbed."

Countess looked behind her. Two of the black-suited security guards were behind her. They were still wearing their helmets, and they'd been so quiet she hadn't known they were walking a few steps behind her. Countess didn't know if it was their training or the equipment, but she was impressed.

The guards nodded to the Baron. Then, when Countess and the Baron went into the room, they took their places on either side of the door.

The door closed with a final thunk behind her. Whatever came next, there would be no going back.

9

The room was claustrophobically small. A few overhead, orange-tinted electric lights cast eerie shadows on the dark green walls. Despite the cramped space, Countess found the color comforting, a welcome change from the bland, gray hallway outside. The only things in the room were a small desk and chair against the back wall and two men standing in front of it at parade rest.

Both were dressed in intelligence officer field gear. Countess immediately recognized one of them as the man from the armored carriage. He had cleaned up well, she noticed. She nodded to him, and he returned the gesture. The other man, whom she didn't recognize, looked somewhat younger and clearly not a field agent. It was the way he carried himself—nervous and unsure, his eyes never settling on any one thing.

Baron Greystone stood with his hands behind his back, looking at each of them in turn. "You're all here because the Kingdom of Yorke needs your help. This is a situation of dire need, and King Leopold himself tasked me with assembling this team. Consider yourselves at the top of a very short list. You're some of the most capable operators in the intelligence community. But don't let that go to your heads. Some, or even all of you, might not survive this mission."

The Baron paused for a moment. "Some of you have met, if only a short time ago. But for everyone's benefit, I will do a short round of introductions. Countess Ella Wellington is to be your team leader."

Countess's eyes widened, and she started to sweat. She was not a team leader and did not want that responsibility. Infiltrators mostly worked alone, only worrying about themselves. She sometimes worked with others, but it was mostly in a one-on-one way. Being in charge of two other people was the last thing she wanted.

"Um, Sir…" she began.

"Please hold all comments and questions until the end," the Baron shot her a stern look.

Countess looked away, feeling dejected.

"Countess has been with the intelligence community for over twenty years and has over one thousand successful missions under her belt."

Lin looked at Countess and made an exaggerated "wow" face. Countess frowned and shook her head at him.

"Her royal title," the Baron continued, "is a result of her retirement from the Intelligence Corps, and you WILL show her the respect of that title." He looked at Countess, "My apologies for cutting your retirement short. The needs of the kingdom, you understand."

Countess suppressed the sting. She had worked for that retirement. Earned it with blood, sacrifice, and ghosts she still dreamed about.

"Yes, sir," said Countess. "It is an honor to serve."

"Very good." The Baron looked at Lin and Vance. "Countess is the best infiltrator in the kingdom and a natural choice for this mission."

The Baron looked at Lin. "Lieutenant Lin Hurst is an assassin in good standing with the Intelligence Corps." Lin stood at attention and pushed his chest out in a slightly exaggerated manner. Countess did not find it flattering.

"He's a 10-year veteran," said the Baron, "and comes highly recommended. He's a weapons expert and will represent the main fighting force of your group."

"Lieutenant Vance Sherwood," said Baron Greystone, "is an expert in technology and security systems. He has also been with the corps for over ten years. His analysis and support have resulted in over 500 successful operations in Saug territory."

Vance stood at attention and Lin went back to parade rest. Countess noticed that Vance was smiling ear-to-ear and blushing.

"His knowledge of current civilian and military equipment, as well as his research into ancient systems, should prove extremely valuable. There is no finer support element I could attach to your team."

Baron Greystone stood at attention. "At ease." Then he went back to his usual hands-clasped-behind-his-back posture. Everyone relaxed. Countess looked at her new teammates and nodded approvingly. Lin and Vance nodded back. Lin looked on edge. Countess made a mental note to keep an eye on him—zeal like that could get people killed. Vance, on the other hand, looked nervous and slightly ill.

"Everyone fall-in behind me, and I'll bring you to our briefing room."

10

Countess followed the Baron, and Lin and Vance walked behind her. The hallway was very long, and Countess was grateful when they finally turned into a large stairwell. They walked down one level and into a wide, open space with outward-angled glass observation windows around its periphery. Countess could see only black outside the windows. A sign over the entry to the area said: "Logistics Management / Operations / Observation."

The room was enormous—at least a hundred feet wide, dimly lit and humming with quiet energy. Control panels ringed the periphery, each embedded with seating and complicated arrays of knobs, switches, and glass panes. There were also what looked like rectangular panes of black glass at eye level, if one were seated at the control panel. Above the observation windows and completely encircling the room were more of the glass surfaces.

In the middle of the room was dominated by a large, circular table. The side of the table was brushed gray metal, and the top was black glass two inches thick. As Baron Greystone neared the center of the room, the entire area magically sprang to life. Countess was temporarily blinded and held a hand above her eyes. The entire ceiling seemed to be composed of square white lights. And all of the shiny black rectangles were now showing bright, moving pictures.

"Whoa," Countess whispered, shielding her eyes from the sudden glare.

Lin was so surprised, he actually pulled a sword from his belt and went into a defensive stance. Vance laughed. "It's okay, guys. This is all perfectly normal." He held out his hands, palms down, and made a slow, patting gesture. "The lights and systems here are automated. They power up in response to our presence."

"How is that possible?" said Lin.

"I've seen traps that do that kind of thing," said Countess. "But there's usually a tripwire or some other mechanical device involved. I see nothing like that here."

"It's a bit more sophisticated than that," said the Baron. "There's no time to explain the intricacies of everything you see today." The Baron's eyes went to each of their faces. He seemed to be watching them very carefully, gauging their reactions to what they were seeing.

Countess looked around the room. There was motion everywhere, and it was hard to know what to concentrate on. Everything seemed to be fighting for her attention. The world outside the observation windows slowly brightened to a warm yellow glow. Countess took several steps over to the nearest window and looked out. She jumped back, stunned. There was a cavernous gulf of space below them. The room they were standing in seemed to be suspended above a vast cave, a square cylinder that seemed to extend down to infinity.

"My god!" said Countess. "It's enormous!"

"This is the control center for a large warehouse," said the Baron. "Four warehouses, actually, and they're all directly beneath our feet."

Lin, who was standing next to Countess, looked down into the warehouse. "Whoa!" he said, his eyes wide. "Nope. No way. That's crazy."

Countess smirked. The assassin who feared nothing had just found a limit.

Vance was more confident. He strode over to the window and bent over. "You guys are just being—" he jumped back. "Okay, yeah! That is…really far down."

"If you'll all join me here," said the Baron. He looked annoyed at them. "We can begin."

Countess, Lin, and Vance gathered at the circular table. The Baron touched something on the black surface, and the area above it was suddenly filled with shapes that seemed to be made of colored light.

"Nice," said Vance. "This is a really good quality holographic display! The best I've ever—" He noticed the Baron was staring at him. "—sorry." Vance bowed his head and said no more.

Countess was amazed. Her eyes danced around the bright and beautiful pictures. The display was showing what looked like a topographical map of the area surrounding Greystone Barony. Then, the Baron touched the table, and the view shifted. The small, irregular circle that was the Barony outer bailey zoomed upward and took center stage.

Countess smiled. She looked at Lin. His eyebrows were raised so high, she thought they were going to detach and fly away.

"As you all know," said the Baron, "earlier this evening, Greystone Barony was attacked by pagan forces. They breached the gatehouse, killed several guards, and proceeded to infiltrate Intelligence Headquarters."

The view zoomed again. This time, the barony keep was the focus. The view rotated and zoomed to its front entrance.

"The pagans entered here, then proceeded to kill more guards and staff."

The view changed to a flat, plan-view map, with each level like a layer in a sandwich. The top and bottom layers sheared off and disappeared from view. Only one slice remained, the map of the ground floor. It angled itself to face them.

"Once inside, they made their way to my office, leaving traps of various types—most were spectacularly lethal. Countess disarmed most of the remaining ones." The Baron looked at Countess. "Thank you, Countess."

Countess smiled but felt uncomfortable during this part of the briefing.

"Once my office was breached, they opened my panic room and stole the most valuable thing in it: one half of a powerful weapon."

The Baron looked at each of them meaningfully, then he bent over and touched the table again. The view changed. There was now a large ring hovering above the table. It seemed to be slowly rotating. Except, it wasn't. The outer surface of the ring was a moving picture of stars. Behind the stars were gas clouds of various colors.

"Beautiful," said Vance.

Lin whistled softly.

"Beautiful and lethal," said Baron Greystone. "This is one of the

Rings of Callifrey. By itself, harmless. But together with its sister ring, it forms a weapon of divine temper, capable of destroying an entire kingdom."

"How could something so small be so destructive?" said Lin.

"We don't know," said the Baron. "It's ancient technology, highly advanced. It set a precedent in military weapon systems even in the advanced age in which it was made."

"I can definitely see that," said Vance. "Even displaying moving images on something that small…that's incredible."

Countess sort of understood Vance's meaning, if only by context. She looked at the Baron. He was smiling at Vance, but there was something more there. It was only there for a split second, but it seemed like Baron Greystone was trying not to laugh.

"And how about a power source?" said Countess. "I know about metal-acid batteries from my advanced systems training, but I've never seen anything this advanced. There would have to be a battery inside this, right?"

The Baron frowned. "The technology inside the rings is highly…compressed, I guess you could say. I'm sorry I don't have more decisive answers for you."

The Baron took a moment to look seriously at each of them in turn. "It is obvious that the pagans don't have the other ring. Otherwise, they would have used it here tonight. And their quick departure seems to indicate they know where the sister ring is located."

Countess looked at Lin. He was hanging on the Baron's every word. Vance looked concerned, and slightly stunned. She might have to talk to him later, ensure his head was in the game.

"Your mission," said the Baron, "is to prevent the pagans from acquiring the Rings of Callifrey, at all costs. Bring them back here, so they can be properly disposed of. The pagans themselves are expendable."

The Baron touched the table again. The map reappeared, zoomed out and centered on the Hud river.

"Your team will meet with my contact named Hollymane in the Forbidden Land. She will—"

Vance timidly interrupted. "I'm sorry, sir. Did you say…the

Forbidden Land?"

"Yes. The ordinance preventing entry is lifted for you three only. You will each receive my mark. The guardians at the crossing will allow you to pass."

Countess looked at Lin. He seemed impressed.

"I've always wanted to go there," he said.

"Trust me," said the Baron. "You don't."

Another touch of the holographic table, and the map panned and zoomed again. A red line extended out from Greystone Barony and moved toward the Hud river.

"You will travel on foot to this location." A red dot punctuated the spot beside the river. "You will meet the guardians at the river, present my mark, and they will ferry you across to the Forbidden Land. From there, your team will be on your own. Be careful." The red line made a left turn and traveled along the river north, then it made a right turn and went across the river. Another dot was placed on the other side of the Hud river, and then the line disappeared onto a huge gray area marked "Forbidden Land."

"Once inside the Forbidden Land," said the Baron, "you will locate Hollymane. She is in a medical facility somewhere inside the ancient city."

"City?" said Lin. "There's a city in there?"

The Baron looked at Countess. "Yes."

Countess looked at Lin and shook her head. He shrugged.

"The sign on the building Hollymane is in will be labeled: 'Labcourse'. Repeat the name with me."

"Labcourse," they all said in unison.

"Very good," said Baron Greystone. "Hollymane will give you powerful weapons with which to fight the pagans. You need them. You've seen the pagans' destructive capabilities already."

The Baron pressed something on the holographic display table, and the map disappeared. He then turned around to face them.

"To review: Your team will travel a short distance to the guardians, who will ferry you to the Forbidden Land. Once inside, locate Hollymane and accept the weapons she gives you. Track down the pagans and prevent them from getting the Rings of Callifrey. Return them here. That is all."

The Baron looked at them and smiled, as if a large weight had been lifted from him. "But before I dismiss you, I have a gift for each of you. A small token of my appreciation."

11

Countess, Lin, and Vance looked at each other with interest.

"Dinner and rest!" said the Baron.

"Ha ha!" said Lin. "I'll take it."

"Thank you, sir," said Countess. She looked at Lin scornfully. "We are honored by your hospitality."

The Baron brought them to the far wall of the Logistics Center, where he pressed a button on the wall. A pair of doors opened, revealing a room which seemed to be nothing more than a cylinder of glass.

Baron Greystone stepped in and Countess's team followed. The doors closed behind them.

Countess's stomach dropped suddenly. Vance actually screamed like a child, and Lin reached out to steady him. "Steady on!" he said.

The glass cylinder dropped out of the bottom of the Logistics Center and was falling rapidly into the darkness below.

"Don't panic," said the Baron. "This is called an elevator. It's a method of transportation…for going up and down, quickly."

"With respect, sir," said Lin. "You gotta warn a guy before you drop a flaming catapult shot on him like that!"

The Baron looked at Lin, snorted, and then resumed looking outside.

Countess wanted to laugh but couldn't. She was too scared and amazed by what she was seeing. Her heart was beating double-time, and she found herself breathing heavily.

The massive space they were descending in was somehow cavernous and empty, and filled with lots of complex-looking equipment. Machines zipped back and forth around a titanic cube, its rows of stacked boxes glowing with color-coded labels. The boxes had names on the side like: Aventor Aerospace, Molecular Dynamics, Titan Maritime, Keplar Industrial, Vaportech, Rayon-Theta, Mechanism, Vortex, and Global Atomics.

Countess's head was swimming. It was too much visual information, too fast.

"Coming up on your right," said the Baron, "is the one active warehouse stack."

There was a huge whooshing sound, as the elevator went past the active warehouse. Large darkly-colored machines were moving boxes out of the long and deep rows of stacked boxes and were setting them down on top of other boxes which were being stacked on a large open platform nearby.

"The orange platforms are cargo elevators," said Baron Greystone. "They move the boxes up or down, depending on where they're needed. Normally these machines are inactive, but I wanted to give you a little show for the ride."

The elevator reached its destination and came to a sudden halt. Countess felt her weight increase, and she reflexively bent her knees to compensate. The elevator doors opened, and the words "Dormitory Level" were written on the opposite wall in large, black letters.

"Now for your meal," said the Baron. He smiled brightly. "You're going to love this."

Countess's team followed the Baron down a wide hallway, and into a room filled with brown boxes.

"I don't know why," said Lin, "But I was expecting something more…"

"Like a prepared meal?" said the Baron.

"Yeah—" said Lin. He was staring blankly at the boxes. "I mean, yes, sir."

"This is the next best thing!" Baron Greystone reached into an open box and pulled out three shiny, brown packages. He handed one to each team member.

Countess looked down at the package. It had a large circular logo on it depicting a bird in flight, and the word PHOENIX. Below that, were the words: MRE Meal, Ready to Eat. Menu 23 - Southwest Style

Beef and Beans.

"Oh," said the Baron, looking at Countess's package. "You got my favorite!"

"I have no idea what I'm looking at," said Countess.

The Baron smiled. "You'll figure it out. Now! To your rooms! I need you rested for your trip tomorrow. Thank me later."

Baron Greystone led the team to their rooms, which turned out to be quite well appointed, each having its own toilet and shower. Countess had seen rooms like this before, but they were usually reserved for field officers or the very wealthy.

"I'll leave you all here. Enjoy your meal and relax. Get some sleep. You'll need it."

Countess turned to enter her room when the Baron stopped her.

"A word, please, Countess?"

Lin and Vance went into their rooms and closed the doors.

Baron Greystone looked at Countess intently. "I know you're having reservations about this leadership role."

"Yes, sir," said Countess. "I am. I work alone. I've always worked alone—"

"Not always," said the Baron, cutting her off. "You've been sent on many missions where you've had to direct others."

"Well yes, but—"

"Let me finish. Your recent VIP mission. You emancipated that bank owner from the Saug prison outside Kings Town."

"Fernhaven. Yeah, that was…not fun. Why did we have to do that, anyway? Didn't seem like one of my usual."

The Baron smiled, looking uncomfortable. "I owed his wife a favor. Sorry about that."

Countess shook her head and laughed. "Now it all makes sense."

"On that mission," the Baron said, "you had to control and guide him to safety. That's leadership."

"I guess so."

"Trust me, I know that guy personally. You'd have to have powerful skills to get him to do anything!"

"He was a handful," said Countess, "but I see what you mean. I may not be the best team captain, but I will see this through to the end."

"I know you will." Baron Greystone stood at attention and saluted Countess. She saluted back.

The baron turned and walked away. In her room, Countess tore into her Meal, Ready to Eat. After opening the third bag inside a bag inside a bag, she found something the color of rust and the consistency of tile grout. She poked it with a spoon. It jiggled. She gave up.

She laid down on the bed and was asleep in seconds.

Outside her door, the hallway lights dimmed. Somewhere below, machinery stirred.

12

The ruins of Eschaton University loomed ahead, their dark silhouettes clawing at the morning sky. The cracked stone marker at the edge of the woods still bore the name, though half-swallowed by ivy: Eschaton University. Below it, the school's old motto, nearly illegible, read Ex Umbra Lux—From the Shadow, Light.

They had left the safety of Greystone Barony just past dawn. Now, less than an hour later, Countess stood at the treeline, gazing at what remained of the infamous university. Broken towers jutted skyward like teeth. Most of the buildings were gutted, half-swallowed by creeping vegetation, rust-streaked walls, and shattered glass. Yet even in ruin, the place exuded menace. Sculpted angels lined the tops of black spires, many missing wings or heads, as though violently decapitated. Crude graffiti defaced reliefs of biblical battles—seraphs clashing with demons—rendering the entire site a collage of forgotten faith and fractured memory.

As they walked through what remained of the outer campus, broken bricks crunched under their boots. The path took them past twisted lamp posts and defaced statues.

Countess led the team in silence, her every step taut with awareness. The air was still, unnaturally so, and even the birds seemed reluctant to sing. Trees hung over the cracked paths like mourners, their branches brushing the crumbling brick walls of forgotten dormitories and research halls.

The university grounds had been slowly overtaken by nature. Vines choked the weathered gargoyles perched atop Brutalist towers. Moss crept up cracked granite spires, many carved with Latin mottoes and biblical scenes of angels waging war against demons. Creeping rust marked where banners and surveillance cameras once hung. The place had the atmosphere of a cathedral, but built for gods long dead.

"This place gives me the creeps," muttered Lin, glancing up at a statue of a robed figure whose stone face had melted in the rain. "It smells like ghosts."

"You're not entirely off," said Vance. "The locals in Highpoint thought this place was haunted. Paranormal stuff. Disappearances. Lights in the sky. Figures watching from the windows. People said some of the professors weren't human."

"You believe that?" said Countess.

Vance shrugged. "I believe it was funded by Ourobouros subsidiaries and had military contracts no one was allowed to talk about. That alone makes it shady."

"You know what?" said Lin Hurst. "I'm just going to say it. We're walking straight into a trap—I can feel it."

"Whoa there," said Countess. "I've known the Baron for a long time. He's never deceived me or anyone else I know. The worst he's ever done is left a detail out to save me from overthinking a mission. In hindsight, I never resented it."

Countess hoped her confidence in the Baron would reassure Lin, but a part of her worried that she might be wrong. What if the Baron had made a mistake this time? What if she was leading her team into a disaster? She pushed the thought away, focusing on maintaining a calm exterior.

"What about you, Sherwood?" said Lin.

Vance Sherwood said, "Please, just call me Vance."

"Fine, Vaaaance," said Lin. "What's your take? You believe any of this nonsense?"

"I think there's really only one thing to worry about."

"And what's that?" said Countess.

"We don't know anything about these pagans. And I find it very unnerving that the Baron doesn't, either. They hit the Barony, killed a lot of people... and almost killed the Baron, too."

"True," said Countess. "It was brutal and decisive, and it could have been a lot worse. If this had been a Saug invasion force and they had seized the HQ building—"

"Goodbye Yorke Kingdom," Lin muttered.

Countess nodded. "Just about. All they had to do was stay. Claim the Barony as theirs."

"But they didn't," said Vance. "They came for the ring, then left, like the Barony had no value to them at all. That's something to think long and hard about."

"They did leave some people behind," said Countess. "But it wasn't an occupying force. When I interrogated one of them, they said they were left to ensure the main three could get away."

Countess thought back to the interrogation, the fear in the pagan's eyes, the uncertainty in his voice. What kind of enemy were they really up against? Could she protect her team from such a mysterious and deadly threat?

"And what about their weapons?" said Lin. "We don't know what they are, or how they work. This is a huge exposure for us."

"Look, here's what I know," said Countess. "I've been dropped into situations that I didn't completely understand. Situations I thought were hopeless. I'm sure you have too."

Lin and Vance nodded.

Countess continued, "But I trusted the mission team to give me the best intel and tools for the job. And I always came back alive. The Baron's never given me a reason not to trust him."

"Oh, come on, Countess!" said Lin. "Don't you see what's happening here?"

"Of course I do," she said.

Lin grit his teeth. "We're being hung out to dry here! These pagans took out a small army of the Baron's elite guards. Walked through them like they weren't even there. What chance do you think we have?!"

"I think..." said Countess. "That we need to go meet Hollymane. I think there's a lot we still don't know. And I think we need to stick together, and keep a level head about all of this. Because we're about to go in... there." She pointed to the ribbon of dark cloud which loomed above the tree line ahead. "And if the rumors are true—"

"Yeah," said Vance. "That over there... the Forbidden Land... that's death. We shouldn't bicker like this in that place. Not even for a moment."

They continued walking, and the silence between them grew heavy. Countess knew she needed to break it to foster some camaraderie.

"So, Lin," Countess began, her voice steady, "how did you come to be an assassin?"

Lin shrugged, not breaking his stride. "My orphanage, when I was a kid. Some kind of selection program for the intelligence service—"

"Wait," Countess interrupted. "Do you know Oakfield Orphanage?"

"Oakfield?" said Lin. "No. I was at Rockport Orphanage."

"Bracklaven! So we're all orphans?" said Vance. "That's... interesting."

"Very," said Countess. She thought about the implications. She thought back on her own life, and her induction into the intelligence service. It made sense—they could monitor the children, watch them play, and quietly select those who showed resilience and potential. Countess herself was selected at a young age and moved to another orphanage. They were encouraged to play a certain way: climbing and sneaking and hiding. She loved it and liked to show off for the adults. And they encouraged her.

The path curved through the center of campus, taking them past an overgrown courtyard and what remained of the central administration building—a massive Gothic tower with shattered windows and vines hanging like drapes.

They continued past a collapsed amphitheater, its seats now filled with weeds and small trees, and across cracked paving stones engraved with the names of past benefactors. Many of the names had been scratched out or blackened. On the far side of the campus stood a great rotunda, ringed with eight pillars and an elaborate frieze of winged figures locked in battle.

"This used to be the library," said Vance. "A lot of theories about what was stored underneath."

Countess slowed. The ground here felt unstable. Beneath their feet, the earth was slightly sunken, like the ceiling of a hidden chamber waiting to collapse. She marked it mentally but kept walking. There wasn't time to explore.

As they passed the remnants of an old earthwork perimeter,

Countess slowed. Half-buried in the scrub and brush was the oxidized length of a massive artillery piece, propped awkwardly on its original stone base. Most of the display plaque had flaked away, but enough lettering remained for Countess to read the name aloud: "Big Bertha – U.S. Navy Brooke Rifle. Hero of the Hudson, 1864."

Vance brushed moss from the cannon's breech. "This was part of Battery A," he said, his voice soft with awe. "According to records, it sank the Ardent Cooper—a Confederate submarine trying to sneak up the Hudson with explosives. But the artillery crew operating Bertha spotted it. One shot. Breach. Gone."

Lin made a low whistle.

"First sub kill by shore artillery" Vance continued. "And the sub's never been found."

Countess stared at the mouth of the barrel, now crusted with rust and vines. "Maybe it's still down there," she said.

As they neared the northeastern corner of the campus, the buildings gave way to thick woods. The trail narrowed, and the trees closed in like sentinels. But even here, the signs of Eschaton's reach remained— a toppled statue in the underbrush, a half-buried concrete access hatch sealed with rusted bolts, and the occasional whisper of hidden machinery humming beneath the earth.

"Are those ventilation shafts?" asked Lin.

"Yeah," said Vance. "Old connectors. The Phoenix project tried to run a mag-lev train tunnel under here. They never finished it. But some of the service tunnels are still accessible. If you know where to look."

Countess didn't respond. She felt it too—the weight of buried secrets. The University was a mausoleum, a vault of forbidden knowledge. And they were walking through its graveyard.

The team entered an open field covered in thick, tall grass. When they were about halfway through, Lin's head snapped up, his eyes narrowing.

"Hold on. There's something hunting us," he said, his voice low and dangerous.

Countess instinctively moved closer to Vance, her senses on high alert. "What is it?"

Lin didn't answer. He moved like a shadow, slipping into the grass without a sound. Moments later, they heard the unmistakable sounds of a struggle – grunts, a guttural snarl, and the swift, wet sound of a blade meeting flesh.

Vance's face drained of color, his eyes wide with fear. Countess put a reassuring hand on his shoulder, though her own heart pounded in her chest.

A few minutes later, Lin emerged from the tall grass, dragging something large behind him. He approached Countess with a smug grin and tossed a massive head at her feet. The creature's head was grotesque, resembling a mutated dog with huge fangs and powerful jaws, its lifeless eyes still open.

"Done," Lin said simply, wiping blood from his sword. "Child's play. Literally. When I was at the orphanage—not my original one, but the fancy one—they used to send us out in hunting parties for these things."

"What is it?" Vance asked, his voice trembling. "I didn't think things like this really existed…"

Lin shrugged again, sheathing his sword. "No idea. There was no official name for them. We just called them 'Uglies.' This one's a Small Ugly. There are others out there, but they won't mess with us now. I took down the alpha, and now the rest have a free meal."

"Small Ugly?" said Countess. "Are there 'Big Uglies'?"

"And Huge Uglies," said Lin. "That would be what we encountered in the carriage."

"I'll never forget it," said Countess.

She took a drink of water from a canteen in her backpack. Each of them had been issued standard packs: rations, water, a compass, field knife, and a red cloth square bearing the Baron's sigil. Countess had also been given a rough map of the Forbidden Land, but she knew it would be useless once they crossed over. That place defied logic. The map was only there for comfort.

Countess led the team out of the tall grass and into a thin patch of woods on the other side. She knew they were close to their destination. As they passed through the last stretch of woods, the canopy thinned. Sunlight broke through the treetops, dappling the ground. Then the trees fell away entirely.

Countess stepped out of the forest and froze.

In the distance, against the backdrop of a looming cliff and the roiling wall of dark cloud beyond, stood two giant statues. She'd seen a lot of statues in her time, but nothing like these. They didn't belong to Yorke. Or even this century.

13

The Bear Guardians stood on their hind legs, forepaws held out as a warning not to approach the Forbidden Land. They had stood for over two centuries—and it showed. Each towered a hundred feet high and looked like they were carved from dark stone. But on closer inspection, it was obvious that it was just a facade. Patches of the fake stone had fallen away, revealing a corroded metal latticework inside. Black, vertical streaks of weathering and patches of moss and lichen covered their surfaces, enhancing their imposing presence.

Behind the guardians was a sheer drop-off, a slate and shale cliff two hundred feet high, which terminated below at the western bank of the Hud. In the river lay the ruins of an ancient metal bridge. The twisted and rusty metal remains lay draped over several oval concrete pylons, which emerged from the water at regular intervals.

The Forbidden Land, on the opposite side, was a dark and foreboding background for the Bear Guardians, enhancing Countess' sense of dread.

As Countess's team approached, two men dressed in modified Yorke kingdom soldier uniforms emerged from behind one of the statues. Their uniforms were not battle dress but more official or ceremonial in nature. The men had a somber look, and Countess could tell they were not happy to be receiving visitors.

Countess whispered, "These must be the guardians the Baron told us about."

"Come not here, travelers," said the older guardian. "Beyond, lies only death."

"We're here on the Baron's business," said Countess. She presented the Baron's mark.

The guardian looked sad. "Very well," he said. "I do not envy you your task, whatever it is. But if you bear the mark, it must be serious, indeed."

The other guardian, at least twenty years younger than the first, said, "We will escort you to the crossing."

"So," said Lin. "I take it you don't get a lot of people out here."

"Some," said the older guardian. "Most, we turn back. All who cross… never return."

"Great," said Vance. "Very encouraging."

"You mean here," said Countess, trying to keep the team positive. "They never return here. They could just return another way!"

The older guardian suddenly looked older and sadder. "Perhaps."

The guardians took the lead and entered a treacherous switchback trail that hugged the cliff wall down to the river. The ground was dry, but the trail was comprised of loose slate and shale, so the risk of foot slips was ever-present. Close to the bottom, they arrived at a small plateau and took a rest. There was a nice view here of the river. In front of them were the ruins of the bridge, most of which had fallen into the water.

Countess noticed something on the ground, almost hidden in the grass. It was a faded blue sign, its twin rusted, metal posts bent harshly at their base, so the sign itself lay almost horizontal to the ground. It said: "Welcome to Johnson Iorio Memorial Park."

After a snack from their backpacks, they started on the trail again and finished their trek to the river. The morning sun helped them find hand and footholds on the way down, but none of Countess's team relaxed until they reached the bottom.

Not too far from where they had exited the cliff trail, they crossed two parallel metal rails with loose rocks under them. The rails ran far off into the distance, north and south along the river.

"What's this?" asked Countess.

"Old-world tech," said Vance. "They called them trains. They used these rails to transport people and goods."

"Trains," said Countess. "How did they work?"

"They had wheels, like on a cart, that would ride on top of these rails. The wheels had a flange to keep them on track."

"Huh," said Countess.

"Until yesterday, I couldn't talk to you about trains. Forbidden topic—old-world tech. Operational security, and all that."

"So what changed?" said Lin.

"The Baron briefed me before you arrived," said Vance. "Said I could tell you anything you wanted to know."

"That sounds like it could come in handy," said Countess.

"I hope so," said Vance. "Because I can't fight. That's on you guys. I'm useless in that capacity."

"We'll see about that," said Countess. "I might be able to teach you a few tricks." She shot an intense look at Lin.

"I guess…" said Lin, "…I could teach you a few things, too."

Countess smiled.

"Unless you piss me off," said Lin. "In which case, I might let you take a few shots before stepping in." He chuckled.

"I'll… keep that in mind," said Vance.

"We're here," said one of the guardians. Countess saw a small boat moored to a wooden post which had been driven into the shore.

"I will stay here," the older guardian said. "My apprentice will take you across."

Countess watched as the older guardian nodded encouragement to the younger one. But the younger guardian looked frightened and just moments from vomiting.

The team put themselves and their gear into the boat, which between Lin and Vance, they almost capsized twice.

When they were settled, the younger guardian grabbed two short oars which were hidden nearby, got into the boat, and pushed them off from the shore.

Countess turned to look at the guardian who remained behind, but he was gone.

"Where—"

"What?" asked Vance.

"Nothing," said Countess. She had more important things to think about now.

It took about twenty minutes to get across the river. The ruins of two great metal bridges were on either side of the boat. The one on the right was completely destroyed. The foundation piers, and random lengths of rusty metal, rising here and there above the surface, were all that remained. The one on the left fared much better. It mostly stood intact, but some of the top sections had collapsed. One in particular was hanging down almost vertically.

"Know anything about these?" said Countess.

"Not much," said Vance. "The one on the right was called the Mid-Hudson Bridge. Later, they named it the F.D.R. after an important person. Lived in the area, I guess."

"And the one on the left?"

"It started as a train bridge," said Vance.

Countess said, "So, the metal tracks we saw before. They went across on top there?"

"Yes, but later, the tracks were removed, and people used it to walk across. Turned it into a park, or something. 'Walkway Over the Hudson' I think they called it."

"That's twice you used that word," said Countess. "Hudson."

"Yeah, in the old world, that's what they called this river."

The boat landed on the eastern shore.

"Give me your marks," said the guardian. His speech was rapid. He thrust out a hand and made urgent grabbing motions, as if the team were keeping him from relieving his bladder.

"You won't need them in there," he said. He raised his chin, indicating the looming dark cloud on the hill. Countess looked up at it and noted it looked positively colossal now.

Countess noticed his voice had become shaky. His previous cool demeanor was gone. Now he looked like a frightened teenager.

"We will return the marks to the Baron," said the guardian. "This way, he will know we did our job and got you this far."

"Thank you for the ride," said Countess. They all handed their marks to the guardian, then rapidly removed themselves and their gear.

"Take care of each other," said the guardian, as he pushed off from the shore. He was staring at the Forbidden Land and rowing fast.

"Because luck..." He swallowed, "...luck won't help you in this forsaken place. I'll pray for you!"

Countess turned to face the dark wall of slowly swirling cloud. It seemed to be alive, reacting to their presence. As they approached, the fog began to change shape, forming monstrous things, flying tentacled creatures, and lumbering hulks. The shapes stretched and morphed, fading into and out of existence.

Low rumbling sounds and creaks echoed around them, as if massive structures were shifting and groaning under immense pressure. Occasionally, there were otherworldly clicks and scraping sounds that sent shivers down their spines. It was clearly trying to frighten them, and it was succeeding.

Countess stood her ground, her heart pounding. It whispered to her, voices just on the edge of comprehension, promising doom and despair. She clenched her fists, refusing to be intimidated.

Lin drew his sword, eyes scanning the fog warily. "This place is alive," he muttered.

Vance looked like he might be sick. "Are we really going in there?"

"Yes," said Countess firmly. "That's our mission."

The closer they got, the more intense the assault became. Shadows darted around them, and the sounds grew louder. Countess felt a cold sweat break out on her forehead, but she kept moving forward.

Countess was a few feet from the angry surface of the cloud wall, when it turned reflective. But it did not reflect the world around her or Lin or Vance. Only her. She saw her face change. It slowly screamed. Then it morphed into a wrinkled, old hag. Then her face melted off, completely, revealing the skull underneath. From behind, a dark and skeletal hand reached out and grabbed for her shoulder.

Lin turned Countess around. "Hey," he said. "Are you alright? You were standing there for a while."

Countess was now very concerned. She shook her head, trying to forget what she just saw.

"This is just the beginning," she said, steeling herself. "Stay close, and don't let it get to you."

Lin nodded, gripping his sword tighter. "We've got this, Countess. Lead the way."

Vance swallowed hard but managed a determined nod. "I'm right behind you."

Taking a deep breath, Countess stepped into the fog, feeling its cold tendrils wrap around her. It seemed to pulse with life, an ever-present reminder that they were venturing into a place where reality could no longer be trusted. But she had to lead them through it. She had to keep them together, no matter what.

And with that, they disappeared into the mist, leaving behind the guardians, the river, and everything they had ever known.

The Forbidden Land swallowed them whole—and the fog did not part.

ACT II - THE FORBIDDEN LAND

14

The dark, twisted thing was already dead before Sobun beheaded it. Shambling out of the woods, it made a choked, hissing sound. Now, it lay before them in a broken heap. The tidy graveyard looked almost serene under the gray sky—until you noticed the blood staining the grass, or the broken body twitching in the gravel.

"What is it?" Priestess asked.

Ansel's fingers flew over the keyboard, his face set in concentration. "System files call it a Reaper. Some kind of reanimated corpse. Highly advanced technology. Never seen anything like it. Network controlled, designed to operate in groups. This one couldn't, though. Its network card's busted."

"Why are its eyes like that?" Priestess asked.

"The eyes contain a sophisticated array of sensors. They can see, hear, and smell through their eyes. And they see in a lot more of the electromagnetic spectrum than we can."

"What does that mean?" Priestess asked.

"They can see in the dark," Ansel said. "They can see the heat of our bodies."

"They're hunters," Sobun said. "It looks like it was a...person...once."

"It was human," Ansel said. "About seven hundred years ago."

"You're joking," Priestess said.

"Not joking. I wouldn't make this up. It's too crazy. This tech's...god-level, Priestess. Like something out of a nightmare."

Priestess felt a chill run down her spine as she considered the implications of the Reaper's abilities. They were up against something far more dangerous than she had anticipated.

"You said they can operate in groups?"

"Yes, Priestess. I'm seeing formation code here. They can be moved around together, like soldiers. They can perform complex, coordinated maneuvers in small squads or at a battalion size."

"We'll have to avoid groups of these things, then," Priestess said. "They're easy enough to dispatch on their own, but obviously their power lies in numbers."

Priestess took a few moments to scan the vicinity for threats. Sobun was doing the same, his eyes darting around, muscles tense, ready for any sign of movement.

They were in a large, public graveyard. The grounds were well-manicured, with many rows of headstones. They had only encountered the one Reaper, but Priestess couldn't shake the feeling that they were being watched. And she was hearing strange noises in the woods. There were more out there, she was sure of it. And if they were connected, then they could call for reinforcements. Yet another reason to tread lightly in this place of death.

"You said you had something else to tell me?"

"Here," Ansel said. "I've been scanning the local network for others like us."

"And?"

"We were alone…until this afternoon. Got a blip in the Aether's outer perimeter."

"The Dead Zone," Sobun said.

"Yes. I keep forgetting people call it that. Kinda appropriate, based on what I read. I wouldn't want to get caught in that."

"I, too, have heard the stories," Priestess said, smiling at Ansel. "You saved us a lot of time and trouble."

Ansel lovingly patted the black laptop. "This baby is just full of tricks! I just had to tell the Aether we were 'friendly'."

"What about this…blip?" Priestess asked.

"Three contacts. A woman and two men. Heading in this direction."

"Are they armed?"

Ansel displayed several images in quick succession. "Two are. The woman has a decent-sized dagger. One of the men has a longsword. Looks like a warrior. We should move. They're getting closer."

"City dwellers, by the look," Priestess said.

"Military," Sobun said.

"Yes," Priestess said. She looked at Sobun. "Let's assume hostile intent. Still have that Noise Box in your pack?"

"Yes, Priestess."

"Set it up on that small building. And I want tripwires in the treeline. There, there, and there."

Sobun bowed and departed.

"And you," she said to Ansel, "learn all you can about these things. If those city dwellers are coming for us, we'll make them wish they hadn't."

15

Things went bad for Countess and her team even before the hallucinations started. Vance took three steps inside the mist, tripped, and fell on his face. His nose wasn't broken, but they had to wait several minutes for the bleeding to stop. When they started moving again, it was even slower and more deliberate.

The map indicated that they should just go straight. Easy enough, Countess thought. But it wasn't. There seemed to be an unlimited amount of obstacles to climb over or go around. Countess had no idea what most of it was. To her eyes, they were just strange, colorless dark shapes. To add to their problems, the team noticed that their compasses didn't work. They were all stuck pointing North for some reason.

And to add to their navigation problems, Countess's eyes and ears started playing tricks on her. It started slowly but grew into a serious problem over time. After twenty minutes, she stopped the team.

"Guys," Countess whispered. "I don't want to alarm you—"

"You seeing things, too?" said Vance. He looked concerned.

"Yeah, weird shadows or something in the fog," said Lin. "And I keep hearing someone whisper my name."

"So it's not just me," Countess said. "It doesn't seem harmful. But it is distracting."

"Any idea what it is?" said Lin.

"It's like someone playing tricks. Messing with us."

"Yeah," said Lin. "But why?"

"Wrong question," said Countess. "We stay on task. Don't worry about what it is, or why it's doing what it's doing."

"I want to go back," said Vance. His eyes widened, and he stared off into the distance. "This…this is really getting to me. We're not too far in! We could easily—"

"No way," said Lin.

Vance panicked and took off running.

"Damn it!" said Countess. "After him!"

Countess and Lin ran together, but Vance had disappeared into the dark gray mist. Her worst fear was realized. They had gotten separated, and one of her team was out of his mind. Not a good way to start a mission.

Vance tripped and fell again, allowing Countess and Lin to catch up.

When Countess saw Vance again, Lin had him by the front of his shirt and was slapping him repeatedly. Vance was bawling.

"I'm sorry, I'm sorry!" said Vance.

"Stupid idiot," said Lin.

"Guys," said Countess. "Shut up and come over here."

They did. Vance had apparently tripped over the body of a young woman.

"Oh, god!" said Vance. "I didn't…"

"Is she—" said Lin.

"Dead," said Countess. "A long time now, by the look of her." Countess started looking her over, checking for anything useful.

"Here," she said. "Notebook. Looks like a diary. No dates, though. Last entries are…hmmm…not good."

"What is it?" said Lin.

"I'm alone now, and I'm trapped," Countess read aloud. "Haven't seen the others for days. It's isolating us, one by one. I wasn't the first."

"Next entry," she said. "Thirsty. So thirsty. I can't think straight and I can't sleep. It won't let me."

"What does she mean, it?" said Vance.

"Shhh!" said Lin.

"Last entry," said Countess. "It let us all in, but it won't let us out. That's what it does. It waits here like a spider in a web. Waits for the next people to enter its lair. The next victims to torture. Mommy, I'm sorry. Sorry for everything. I should have listened and stayed away from this cursed place. But the Baron needs us to save the kingdom, and...I let him down. Maybe we all did. I hope the others make it, because I don't think I can. I'm too tired. I'm going to try to sleep. Maybe it will let me this last time."

"That's crazy," said Vance.

"No, that's us," said Countess. "That's what will happen to us if we get separated or get turned around in here."

Vance wiped his eyes and walked over to Countess and Lin. Out of the corner of his eye, Vance saw the woman twitch. He looked down at her. Her head turned, then she rotated to face him. Vance's eyes went wide, but he was too horrified to move or speak.

The woman's eyes opened. They were completely black and glossy, and in the centers, where the pupils were supposed to be, a terrible blue glow.

The woman reached out to him with a pale and disfigured hand. "Vaaaaaaaance..."

"Ahhh..." was all Vance could manage.

Countess looked up at him. "Vance? What's wrong?"

Lin was on him. "Hey!" he said, grabbing Vance by the collar. "What the fuck is wrong with you?!"

Vance looked at Lin. "I...the woman, she..."

"The woman what?" said Countess.

"She moved," said Vance. "She reached out for me."

"The fuck she did!" said Lin. He shook Vance hard. "This guy's lost his shit!"

"Hey!" said Countess. "Let him go."

Vance looked down at the woman. She was just lying there in the same position they had found her.

"This place is evil," he said. "...and cold. Why am I so cold?"

"Cold?" said Lin. "Is he serious? I'm having hot flashes!"

Countess stood and looked at them. Lin was sweating, and Vance was hugging himself, shivering.

"Alright, let's all just take a moment," said Countess. "We know something is making us see and hear things. It was confirmed by the woman's diary. Maybe it can affect the temperature, too."

"Is that possible?" said Lin.

"I don't know," said Countess, "and I really don't care. I just know we have to get out of here, or we're going to end up like her."

"So, what's the plan?" said Lin.

"Same as it was before," said Countess. "With one update. We stay calm, and ignore everything unless it's physically blocking our path. In which case, we go around, but keep our orientation. With me?"

Lin and Vance nodded.

When they started walking together, more-or-less in their original direction, the hallucinations began again in earnest. Countess lost track of time, but it seemed like they had been walking for hours.

What started as whispers were now voices of men and women, beckoning for her to save them, or to follow them off in the wrong direction. She was sure Lin and Vance were hearing them too. Most of the dark shapes they had been avoiding turned out to be mirages—not there at all. The team soon learned to ignore what their eyes and ears were telling them, and just walked forward.

***

They staggered forward slowly, almost completely blind. The spinning tornado around them picked up speed and ferocity, a howling vortex of chaos. Countess led the way, with Lin gripping the back of her shirt, and Vance behind him doing the same.

"Turning and turning in the widening gyre," intoned a deep, god-like voice that shook the very air around them.

"What the hell is that?" shouted Lin, his voice barely audible over the roar of the storm.

"I don't know!" Countess yelled back, her voice strained with determination. She trudged on, each step a battle.

"The falcon cannot hear the falconer," the voice continued, echoing through the tempest.

"I want to go home," Vance said feebly, his voice trembling with fear.

"Things fall apart; the centre cannot hold," the voice boomed, as the tornado's ferocity reached a terrifying crescendo.

There was an earthquake, or what felt like one. Countess lost her footing and fell to her knees. Lin and Vance fell forward, almost collapsing on top of her.

In a feat of amazing strength, Lin picked up Countess, her feet dangling for a moment.

"I'm alright!" said Countess.

"It's getting desperate!" said Lin.

The sound of the tornado was almost deafening, and it had turned very dark. Countess could not see the ground in front of her. It was just a swirling mass.

She held her hands out in front of her and took three plodding steps. Then, her hands broke through. It was as if she was underwater, pushing her hands up through the surface and into the air.

The air felt calm on her hands, but the torrent around her forearms felt like it was threatening to rip her hair out.

"I think we're almost through!" she said. "A few more steps!"

Then, without warning, the storm dissipated and fell away. The loud sounds diminished, and their vision returned. The voices in Countess's head went silent, and there were no phantom images.

They were standing in a small park. Several strange buildings stood nearby. Countess couldn't see very far—maybe fifty feet ahead. The team was still in the Forbidden Land, but the fog was lighter here, both in color and density. Countess could see the dim outlines of several more buildings in the distance.

16

The Baron's map had instructed them to find something called a Post Office, whatever that was. Countess and her team found it easily enough, as it was clearly labeled, and the building was in perfect condition. The streets were eerily immaculate, the windows clean, and the air smelled faintly of antiseptic.

"Guys," said Vance, his voice hushed with awe. "I think this is what the old world looked like."

"Yeah," said Lin, scanning the surroundings. "It's all preserved. Not a single broken window or rusted metal."

"Maybe the mist protects everything in here somehow," said Countess, her eyes narrowing as she surveyed the area. The silence was unnerving, amplifying every footstep.

"I can't see why," said Vance, shaking his head. "Who would want to live like this?"

"Maybe no one," said Lin. "There's nobody here."

"Well," said Countess, pointing across the street, "except for whatever those things are." A small group of white-furred animals were grazing. One stood on its hind legs, hissed at them, and then scampered off, followed by the others.

"So the Lab should be just behind here," said Vance.

"Yeah," said Countess, consulting the map. "It shouldn't be too far."

They walked around to the back of the Post Office, and Vance cried out in disbelief.

"Are you kidding!"

"Keep your voice down!" whispered Countess, her eyes darting around.

"Look at them all!" said Vance, his eyes wide. "Automobiles. I think this is what they called a parking lot!" He pressed his face to the glass of one vehicle. "Why would anyone make chairs out of animal skin and metal?"

"Hey!" said Countess. "No! Don't touch anything."

"They could have traps," said Lin.

"Exactly," said Countess. "Stay on task—look! There's LabCourse!"

"Wow," said Vance, noticing the illuminated sign. "They have power."

The LabCourse building, unremarkable except for its fancy sign, stood across the parking lot. The sign read: LabCourse - Testing All Your Body Fluids Since 1975! Countess led the team to the front doors, which opened easily and silently.

Countess was amazed. "Look at how well this is machined. I've never seen a door this well made." She caught herself. "Sorry!"

Vance and Lin chuckled.

"Countess likes doors," said Lin. "Who knew?"

"Don't worry," said Vance. "Your secret's safe with me." Countess punched him playfully and smiled.

Inside, the reception area was pristine, with large sofas, a long counter, and several desks behind it. Strange objects cluttered the desks, but there was no dust, and the room was well lit. High windows let in the gray light from outside. A child's doll lay on the counter.

Vance plopped onto one of the sofas. "Oh, that feels nice." He threw his head back and sighed.

"Hello!" Lin called out. "Anyone here?"

"Hollymane!" said Countess. "Baron Greystone sent us!"

Silence.

"Well," said Countess. "This is great. We come all this way to be stood-up. Vance, help us look for clues."

"There's nothing here," said Lin. "Just this stupid doll."

"Doll, yes," said a voice. "Stupid, no."

"What the—" said Lin, his hand reaching for his sword.

"Hollymane," said the voice, cheerful and female.

"Wait," said Vance, sitting up. "Where are you?"

"Here! On the counter."

Countess approached the counter and leaned over to inspect the doll. It looked worn, with scratches, singed hair, and a faded blue dress with white lace trim. "You're kidding," she said.

"I'm not kidding." The voice did seem to come from the doll. "I'm going to get up now, so don't panic."

The doll stood up on the counter and looked at each of them.

"Whoa, whoa, whoa!" said Lin, drawing his sword. "What is this sorcery?"

"Cool!" said Vance, his eyes wide with fascination.

"How is this possible?" said Countess. "Magic?"

"No magic," said Hollymane. "Just clever robotics and software."

"I...don't know what that means," said Countess. "But I'll take your word for it, Hollymane."

"It's technology," said Vance, peering closely at the doll. "Pretty advanced, too, to fit in such a small package."

"Indeed," said Hollymane, swatting Vance away. "And please, call me Holly."

"Wait, so...how—" began Lin.

"I'm sorry I can't join you in person," said Holly. "I'm sick. I can't go outside. This doll allows me to get around."

"How are you sick?" asked Vance.

"Radiation. I grew up in an area with a high concentration. I became...disfigured. You wouldn't want to see me anyway," she said softly. Then, almost too quickly: "But Gumdrop gets me out and about!"

"Oh, no," said Countess. "That's terrible."

"Not really," said Holly. "I don't mind staying at home, and thanks to Gumdrop here, I get to have lots of adventures."

"I'm sorry. Gumdrop?" said Lin.

"Gumdrop is the doll," said Holly.

"Oh!" said Countess. "I see."

"Look, I know why you're here. The Baron sent word that you were coming. And I know you may be questioning how a child's doll can help you."

"The thought did cross my mind," said Vance.

107

"You're in good hands," said Holly. "I have very powerful equipment for you. Weapons of exceptional potency." Holly laughed. "And you can put that pig sticker away, Lin. You won't need it for now."

Lin sheathed his sword. "Fine," he said. "What's a pig?"

"Forgive me," said Holly. "Pigs were domesticated animals in the old world. Sadly, like many animals, they don't exist anymore."

"You know about the old world?" said Countess.

"Quite a bit, yes."

"How old are you, Holly?" asked Vance.

"Old."

Countess, Lin, and Vance exchanged glances but said nothing.

"Did you make Gumdrop, or…" began Vance.

"I found it," said Holly. "Where I used to work. It was in a lab, though not like this one, where they made such things."

Holly paused, looked down at the counter, her hands resting lightly on its surface.

"Look, I know you have a lot of questions, but we have to get started. Those pagans are on their way to get the other half of the weapon, as I'm sure the Baron told you. If they assemble it, they could destroy the kingdom, and we can't let that happen."

"So," said Lin. "Where can we get our hands on these weapons?"

Holly said, "You'll find them buried—in a graveyard, of course."

17

The sky darkened as the sun slipped beneath the horizon, casting long shadows over the perfectly preserved streets of the Forbidden Land. Countess led her team cautiously, Holly perched on her shoulder, her wide eyes glowing faintly, scanning the thickening fog ahead.

"Why not just meet us at the graveyard?" Countess asked, stepping carefully over a cracked but otherwise pristine sidewalk.

"Tried that," Holly replied. "People get lost and die in here," Holly said. "It's safer to meet you on this side of the Dead Zone."

"The Dead Zone was insane," Vance muttered behind her.

"That was tame," Holly said. "The Aether is only set to Defense mode. It has two higher settings you don't want to experience."

"Aether?" Lin echoed, puzzled.

"The fog," Holly explained. "It's part of a battlefield command and control system—nanotech, linked drones, surveillance, psy-ops. The system was built to protect this place."

"Protect from what?" Vance asked.

"Enemies. Russia. China. The future. Reality," Holly said, ticking them off on tiny fingers. "Take your pick. But if you're not listed as friendly, the system sees you as hostile."

"So… us," Vance sighed.

"The Dead Zone is just its outer ring," Holly continued. "In terms of lethality, Defense mode is about a two out of ten."

They continued southward, the mist curling tighter around them as they reached a broad boulevard lined with tall, modern buildings— eerily intact, lit from within by sterile white lights. Overhead, a cracked sign hung from a sleek archway:

Welcome to Archangel Medical Center

"Archangel," Countess said under her breath.

"One of Phoenix's favorite covers," Holly confirmed. "People came here to be healed. Some got better. Some disappeared. Some are still here...in a way."

They walked in silence past a large building labeled Psychiatric Health Center – Building 20. Its outer lights flickered slowly, casting rhythmic shadows across the empty lobby beyond the glass. Next came the Women's Health Center and a towering steel cross marking the Spiritual and Religious Center (Building 6). Banners still clung to its sides like old skin, bearing faded words: Faith Beyond Healing and From This Life To The Next.

Countess glanced up at a nearby tower:

Building 12 – Emergency, Surgery, Oncology

A motionless gurney sat in the entry vestibule. A wheelchair leaned against the wall, still facing the door like someone had once been waiting.

"It's like the world stopped and left the lights on," Lin whispered.

"Not quite," Holly said. "Lights still work. So do the doors. The cameras never stopped watching. But no one lives here anymore."

They turned onto a cracked drive near Building 11 – Transplant Center. A faded patient drop-off sign swayed in the wind, just above a long-shuttered shuttle bus. A nearby sign read:

Restricted Access – Poughkeepsie Rural Cemetery & Utility Maintenance Only

"This is our path," Holly said. "Down this road."

The fog thinned slightly as they passed the final boundary of Archangel's domain. Ahead, iron gates jutted from heavy stone pillars. The rusted arch above them read:

Poughkeepsie Rural Cemetery – Est. 1853

Countess stopped at the threshold. The chill was deeper here, and the fog felt... heavier somehow. Pressing down. Coiling.

"Why does a medical center connect to a graveyard?" Vance asked.

"Convenience," Holly said.

Nobody responded.

Holly jumped down from Countess's shoulder and began to lead the group.

Suddenly, the fog shifted. A distant hum rose above them.

"Drone," Holly whispered.

They ducked behind a moss-covered monument as a matte-black scout passed overhead, its red and white lights blinking in rhythmic intervals. It hovered briefly, scanning the area with a piercing blue beam before drifting away toward the north. The silence that followed was worse.

"How did you know it was coming?" Countess asked.

"Gumdrop's wired into old Phoenix systems," Holly said, tapping her doll's forehead. "We pick up all kinds of things."

They continued into the cemetery, flanked by rows of weather-worn headstones and statues cloaked in ivy. Countess's boots crunched gravel as she stepped over a fallen stone angel, its face eroded into a skull-like mask.

"This is it. The cemetery," Holly said, voice low and even now uncertain. "The place we're going... it's deep inside. And it's watched."

"Watched by what?" Lin asked.

"Reapers," Holly said. "If we're lucky, we'll only have to fight a few."

Countess felt a familiar tension rise through her chest. "Reapers. What do they look like?"

"You'll know when you see them," Holly said. "They have glowing blue eyes. If you fight one, aim for those eyes."

She stepped ahead into the fog.

Countess followed.

And then the real danger began.

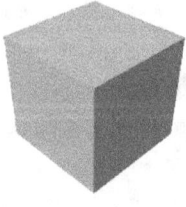

18

The team wound its way into the depths of the graveyard, and their dread grew with each step. Countess could sense movement out in the periphery, and it was unnerving. Rustling leaves and distant animal sounds interfered with her attempts to isolate threats, and the chilly night air added to her apprehension.

She felt exposed. They passed rows and rows of gravestones on either side, but they were small and useless to hide behind. All the grass was short, impossible to hide in. The team maneuvered in the open, trusting Holly to avoid trouble. The only respite came when they found cover next to mausoleums or hid in a small copse of trees.

Despite the cemetery's small entrance, Countess was really starting to get a sense of how big this place was.

Holly whispered, "Okay, stop here."

They were now resting in a small stand of trees. Countess caught the scent of brackish water nearby; a pond or a swamp.

"I've been avoiding the Reaper patrols so far, but we're getting close to the mausoleum. They're a lot more concentrated here."

"If they're guarding it, it must be special," said Countess.

"It is," said Holly.

"Our weapons are in there?" asked Lin.

"Yes," said Holly, "among other things."

"Well, now you've piqued my interest," said Vance. "Secret treasure guarded by monsters in a graveyard. What's not to love?" He was trying to be funny, but his trembling voice revealed how frightened he was.

"The fact that these monsters can kill you quite efficiently," Holly said, her tone matter-of-fact. "Let's keep going. We're almost there."

The path led the team near a small lake, confirming Countess's suspicions about the source of the smell. Holly took them off the path and into the woods. They were heading west now, toward the river, and had to move much slower to keep their progress quiet. A single broken stick underfoot could bring the Reapers down on them.

Holly was on the ground, leading the team through the darkness, and she was really fine-tuning their movements. They seemed to be tracing a zig-zag pattern through the woods, and to Countess's frustration, at a snail's pace. One time they even moved back several hundred feet to avoid something only Holly seemed to detect.

Countess saw an opening in the woods up ahead. There was a fairly large, white mausoleum in what looked like a wide, circular clearing.

"I think luck is on our side," whispered Holly. "We might be able to make a run for—"

A terrible shrieking sound started repeating from the direction of the mausoleum. At the same time, a flashing light pulsed brightly from its roof.

"Guys—," said Vance. "I think I just stepped on something."

And then the shrieking began.

"Shit," said Lin. "It's a trap!"

"They're going to swarm the entrance," said Holly. "We'll never get in!"

"Be right back," said Countess. She ran hard into the clearing, leaving the team behind.

"Countess!" Lin whisper-shouted after her.

Countess didn't see anything at the corners of her vision. She was concentrating on getting to the mausoleum as fast as she could.

On the front of the building, above the entrance door, was the word "CRANE". To either side were three-foot-tall, stone lion statues. She climbed onto the back of the nearest one, then carefully stood on its head. While facing the roof of the mausoleum, she crouched, then launched herself up, catching the edge of the roof with her fingers.

The mausoleum had small windows set high in the wall, which she used to get leverage. She gingerly hooked a foot into the bottom of a window frame and pushed off while lifting herself onto the roof. It was a little clumsy and slow, if she was honest—not her finest work.

Countess moved over to the flashing and blaring source. It looked like a small handmade wooden box with strange electrical components attached to it. She squatted down to grab it.

It was then that Countess saw the Reapers for the first time. Three groups emerged from the fog on the edge of the forest.

They were terrible, dark and shambling things; gaunt, sexless, and without clothing. Holly had been right. They were human-like, but certainly not human. And their eyes! Their eyes were inky-black, but the surface shimmered like small pools of oil. And in the center of each eye was a glowing blue light.

What are these things? Countess thought, her heart pounding in her chest. Holly had warned them, but seeing them in the flesh... they were even worse than she imagined. Why didn't she tell them exactly what they were up against? A shiver ran down her spine as she took in their formation. Each group moved with unnerving precision, like they were controlled by a single mind. They weren't a mindless horde, they were organized hunters.

The Reapers moved in formations shaped like triangles, the tips of which were pointing in her direction. Each triangle was comprised of ten to fifteen Reapers.

There was no time to think about it now. She had to act, and fast. The small box was quite light. Countess picked it up and hurled it as hard as she could over the tops of the trees and into the woods to the north. She hoped she had her directions right. The last thing she needed was to accidentally throw it in the direction of her team.

Her gambit worked. The Reaper formations stopped, reoriented themselves, and disappeared back into the woods.

Countess heard Vance scream, but it was cut short. There was a sudden flash of blue light from the tree line, accompanied by a sharp, electrical snap—like a thunderclap being forced through a keyhole.

"What the—" Countess rubbed her eyes. There was now a slowly-fading black spot in her vision.

Countess lowered herself down off the roof of the mausoleum and sprinted back to her team.

She arrived to chaos. Lin had five Reapers surrounding him, and he was using his sword and dagger to fend them off.

Vance was on the ground, motionless. She could see blood on his face and clothes. Two Reapers were standing over him, but hadn't noticed her arrival. She pulled her dagger and crept toward them, remembering what Holly had said about their vulnerability.

"Hey!" she said as she advanced on them.

One of the Reapers turned its head to face her, and she struck hard and fast towards its right eye. She had the element of surprise, and her strike was true. Her dagger's blade sank to the hilt. The thing slumped to the ground, like something mechanical inside it turned off.

"Remember the eyes!" she said to Lin.

"On it," he said in return. His voice was cold and controlled, and his movements were rapid and precise.

The other Reaper swiped at Countess with long and sharp talons, but she managed to dodge in time. She countered, but her thrust landed wide of the mark. Not wanting to let it take another swing at her, she leaned back and kicked it hard in the chest with the ball of her foot. The Reaper was sent reeling backward and off balance. It stumbled, lost footing, and landed on its back. Countess reoriented the dagger in her hand so the blade was emerging from the bottom of her fist. She jumped on the Reaper's chest and dropped her fist like a hammer, piercing its eye with a force that cracked its skull.

Countess looked to Lin. He had already dispatched three of the Reapers. That left two; one for each of them.

Countess kicked at the closer one. It faced her, made a hissing sound, and swiped hard at her face. She ducked to the side, but it slashed her shoulder and upper arm. Each talon was like a surgeon's scalpel, and she bled from the cuts. Countess had received wounds like this in the past, and she could ignore the initial pain—though not for long.

While the Reaper's arm was extended from its attack, Countess shifted sideways and hooked her own arm around it. Locked together, Countess and the Reaper were brought almost face to face. She could smell its awful breath, like some foul, rich soil. It opened its maw to menace her as she drove her blade home into its eye socket.

When Countess looked at Lin, he was standing proudly with his arms crossed. He was smiling, and his weapons were sheathed. All the Reapers were down.

"Not bad, Countess," he said. He started to clap lightly.

Countess bent over to catch her breath. She was exhausted but determined. "All in a night's work for you?!"

"I discovered that cutting their heads off works, too."

"Good to know," said Countess, shaking her head. "Where's Holly?"

"Here I am," said Holly, emerging from behind a tree. Countess noticed an odd flicker in her eyes. She seemed to realize how that looked to the team and said, "Well, I can't fight the Reapers! You want me to bite their ankles, or something?"

Countess suddenly remembered Vance and ran over to him. He was alive but cut badly on his face and upper body.

"Pulse is strong, but shallow," Countess muttered, pressing her fingers to his neck. "He's alive. We've got minutes, maybe less."

This is my fault, she thought, feeling a pang of guilt. I led them into this. If only I had been faster... Could I have prevented this? She pushed the thought away. There was no time for self-doubt now.

"We have to get him inside," said Holly. "There are medical facilities in there."

"There?" said Lin. "In that little house?"

"You'll see!" spat Holly. "Now quickly! More will come!"

Countess and Lin carried Vance's body toward the mausoleum, but as they reached the door, two groups of Reapers emerged from the forest. Why didn't Holly warn them about the Reapers in more detail? Countess wondered, feeling a shiver of mistrust. What more could she be hiding from them? And why is she so calm in the face of this danger?

"Get in!" said Holly. "Now."

They moved Vance's body inside and Lin went back to close the door.

The Reapers were right outside. They apparently didn't know how to operate the doorknob. They started banging hard against the door.

"There!" said Holly, pointing to one of the crypts. "Click the word Ichabod."

"Can't you do it?" said Countess. "You're right there!"

"It's a capacitive sensor... It has to be a human finger," said Holly. "These doll hands won't work. Now hurry!"

"Definitely hurry," said Lin, facing the door. His sword and dagger were in his hands. "These things are gonna break down the door any second."

Countess clicked the nameplate, and there was a loud thunk. The team was knocked off-balance when the entire floor of the mausoleum started moving downward.

"Well, that's a neat trick!" said Countess.

When they had dropped about ten feet, a clear panel slid in place over their heads. As if on cue, the door above burst open and a large horde of Reapers came pouring through. They saw the team below and threw themselves onto the floor, scratching and pounding on the transparent separator. Others dropped on top of them and crawled over them looking for an open spot. They all stared down at the team with those terrible eyes.

"My god," said Countess, "they're like...insects."

"They are," said Holly. "Their control program is partially based on insect swarming behavior."

"They fight like insects, too," said Lin. "People often pause while their allies attack. These things are brute-force, attack all at once. Like a flurry."

"We won't have to worry about them getting through that," said Holly. She pointed upward. "It's six-inch plexiglass."

"Is that good?" asked Lin.

"In this case," said Holly. "It's very good."

The lift came to the bottom of its travel, and the wall in front of them slid sideways, revealing a brightly lit room. Countess was instantly reminded of the area under the Barony, as there were no apparent light sources. She took a deep breath, preparing herself for whatever lay ahead.

"What's this?" asked Lin. He walked over to a large plaque on the wall. It had a large circular logo with the image of a fiery bird, and writing beneath.

It read:

Phoenix Facility 1.1.1.9.5

Eternal Taiga
Hudson Valley In-Processing & Training Center
Poughkeepsie Rural Cemetery Connector – NY Facility 5
Holly said, "Welcome to Eternal Taiga."

19

Countess followed Holly while helping Lin carry Vance's unconscious body. Her muscles burned from the effort, but she pushed through, focusing on Vance's labored breathing.

"We have to stop so we can stabilize Vance," said Countess. "I have some medical training—"

"Don't bother," said Holly, cutting her off. "We're taking him to get fixed now. Won't take long."

Vance was still bleeding quite badly, but Countess didn't think there was any internal damage. A cut artery would be obvious, and Vance wouldn't have survived long if he had one of those. Her own wounds were quite shallow by comparison, and the bleeding had slowed considerably. The sterile, metallic scent of the facility contrasted sharply with the iron tang of blood.

"This place looks pretty advanced," said Lin. "Isn't there anything here we can use to patch him up?"

Holly said, "This is just a decontamination and security mezzanine. Not much here in terms of medical supplies. The actual facility is about a mile below us. We'll be taking an elevator down to it. Don't worry. Almost there."

They proceeded down a main hallway, past offices and corridors branching off to either side. Countess couldn't shake the feeling of being watched, the glass walls and the hum of unseen machinery amplifying her unease. They passed through an area Holly referred to as a "security checkpoint," which had glass walls on three sides with long horizontal slits at about waist height. The first transparent wall in front of them had a note taped to it.

"What the hell is this?" said Lin. He pulled off the note and read it aloud. "If you're reading this, you survived my trap. Congratulations. You're more resourceful than I thought. Now stop following us—first and last warning. If you get in my way, I will kill you. — Priestess Vilma."

"Priestess?" said Countess.

"The pagan woman leading the team, no doubt," said Holly.

"What do we know about them?" asked Countess, her mind racing. Who were these people, and what did they want?

"Not much," said Holly. "Other than the fact that they have some exotic weaponry in their possession. And before you ask, no, I don't know where they got it, what it is, or how it works."

"I just hope the weapons you give us will match what they have," said Countess.

"Offensively? No," said Holly. "But they will make up for it in other ways. Let's keep going."

As they approached, the transparent barriers parted, vertically, down the center and allowed the team to pass. They reached the end of the long hallway, which terminated in a wall with several black metal doors arranged along it.

"These are the elevators," said Holly. "I know you're seeing a lot you don't understand. Don't worry, the answers will come."

"I hope so," said Countess. "This place seems worse than the one under the Barony."

"Both were made by the same group of people. You've probably noticed some similarities."

"In both places I feel similarly uncomfortable!" said Lin. He smiled at Countess, but she was not amused.

"I'm assuming you don't know how elevators work," said Holly. "So here are the basics. Press a button on the wall, up or down. Since we're on the top floor, there's only a down button. The doors open, and there's a small room inside, which we will ride in down to the floor we want to go to."

"A lot better than stairs," said Lin. He was sweating from carrying Vance and getting tired by the look.

"And much faster," said Holly. "The amount of stairs we'd have to traverse would take hours. The elevator will get us there in a few minutes. Countess, can you press the button, please?"

Countess did. The black doors parted, and a small bright and empty room was inside. Holly entered, and Countess and Lin followed with Vance. The doors closed behind them, and they carefully set Vance down on the floor.

"There's a panel on the wall there," said Holly. "We want Level 2: Medical."

"Got it," said Lin. He found and pressed the button.

Countess had a moment of vertigo. She felt weightless for a few seconds, then slowly, her weight returned.

"Wow," said Lin. "That was... faster than falling."

"The carriage moves very fast," said Holly. "You'll get used to it."

"Uh!" said Countess. She still felt like she was falling, and not quite in control. "Feels like my stomach is going to come out of my mouth."

They rode in silence for several minutes, then a kind-sounding woman's voice said, "Approaching next floor."

"Bend your knees a little," said Holly. "Like you've jumped off a short wall and are bracing for landing." They did. There was a sound, like a spoon tapping the side of a glass, then for a moment, Countess felt very heavy. She lost her balance slightly, then righted herself. The doors opened, and the team exited, grateful to escape the strange place.

"This way," said Holly. She walked left past what looked like a long reception desk. They were in another hallway which extended out of sight in both directions from the elevators.

Vance was starting to feel really heavy, and Countess shifted his weight to give her muscles some respite. Vance moaned slightly.

"He might be coming out of it," said Countess.

"Doesn't matter," said Holly. "The bed's smarter than any of us."

"The bed?" said Lin.

"Here we are," said Holly. She walked into a dim room, but the lights brightened in response to her presence.

"Put him up here," said Holly. She pointed to a table with bright blue padding, one of many arranged along the walls of the room.

Countess and Lin carefully placed Vance on the table, then dodged back when a voice said, "Stand clear."

A panel opened on the ceiling over the table, and a clear box with no bottom lowered over Vance.

Vance's eyes opened, and he looked around, frightened.

"Hey!" said Vance, his voice muffled. "Get—" He was interrupted by a small delicate-looking finger, which descended from the top of the box and jabbed him in the shoulder.

Vance's eyes rolled back and closed. Then, several more fingers emerged and began doing various things that Countess didn't quite understand. She honestly couldn't tell if they were helping Vance or hurting him. But whatever they were doing, they were doing it fast.

All Countess could do at this point was trust Holly.

"This will take a while," said Holly. "You should get some rest. You've been through a lot today."

Countess realized that she was, indeed, quite exhausted.

"I'll take you to your rooms," said Holly. "They're just down the hall."

20

Countess woke in a strange room to beautiful music. She felt foggy and light-headed, like she drank too much. She put her hand to her shoulder, where she had been slashed by the Reaper. She found light bandaging there, but she didn't remember receiving them. She didn't remember falling asleep in the bed either, for that matter.

"Hello?" Countess said to no one in particular. The music quickly faded away, and the room began to brighten, filling with a warm, orange glow. She sat up, and the room started to spin.

"Uh," said Countess. She shook her head, and the room righted itself. She swung her feet down to the floor. The bed had been very comfortable. Too comfortable, in fact. It was the kind of comfort that ruined all future beds. She was both grateful and resented it.

"Countess," said Holly's voice. "I'm recording this for when you wake. Look around the room you're in and use what you need to freshen up. When you're done, exit your room and turn right. Walk about two hundred paces and keep your eyes left. I'll be in a dining area with some breakfast for you. Right. Two hundred paces. Left."

Countess liked Holly, but there was something…not right about her. What that something was, she couldn't put her finger on. It was subtle, but it was there.

She got up from the bed and looked around the room. As she stood, the light grew brighter by degrees. The light was like the other rooms and hallways of this facility, in that no lights were visible. Instead, the walls and ceilings themselves seemed to glow. And out of the glow on the walls, soft shadows began to appear. Swaying grass and trees were projected, making the walls seem like they were slightly transparent, frosted glass. It had a calming effect Countess liked.

Everything in the room was shiny, new, and without dust. She didn't know how this was possible and made a mental note to ask Holly about it when she asked her thousand other questions.

There was a small door in the room with hazy, semi-transparent glass. She opened the door and looked inside. Most of the objects she could not identify, but there were a few she did. There was a bar of soap on a small metal shelf and a large metal knob set in the middle of the wall. She had seen something similar in the wealthier homes she had the pleasure of breaking into.

Countess twisted the knob, and a fine mist of water sprayed from a small pipe above her. If she read the label right, the farther she turned it, the warmer the water would get. This turned out to be true, so she set it to a comfortable temperature, slipped out of her clothes, and stepped inside. When she was done, she dressed again and followed Holly's instructions to breakfast.

As Countess walked down the hallway, she couldn't shake the feeling of unease. Holly's voice echoed in her mind, and she replayed the instructions, wondering why everything felt so orchestrated. What's her endgame here? Countess thought. Two hundred paces, then left. So odd and specific. She didn't need to count her steps, and was concerned as to why Holly would give her instructions in this way. Countess continued walking, noting the pristine condition of the facility, and felt a chill run down her spine. It was all too perfect.

Lin and Vance were already sitting at a round table laden with a variety of exquisitely prepared dishes. The dining area was a marvel of automated culinary technology, designed with sleek, futuristic aesthetics. The machinery here exuded a sense of both comfort and sophistication.

Holly was sitting on top of the table with her hands neatly folded in her lap. She smiled when Countess arrived. Countess was delighted to see that Vance was doing well, despite having several long, angry red scars on his face and neck.

"I'm glad you're still with us," Countess said. She smiled at Vance.

He half-smiled back at her. She could tell he was in pain but was taking it well.

"I got cut up bad," Vance said, "but the medical bed patched me up. That thing is truly a miracle of technology."

"Stay closer to me next time," said Lin. "I can't help you if there's a kingdom between us."

"Ok, ok," he said, and then turned his attention back to what he was eating.

"I hope you liked Clair de Lune," said Holly. When Countess looked confused, she said, "The song that played when you woke."

"Oh, yes," said Countess. She sat with them at the table. "Beautiful! I've never heard anything like it."

Countess wondered why Holly chose that particular piece. It was almost as if she wanted to evoke a specific emotional response. Music had power, and Holly seemed to understand that deeply.

"The song was already hundreds of years old when this facility was built," said Holly. "Most people agree that it's one of the finest pieces of music ever written."

"About this facility—" said Countess. "Eternal...Taiga? Do I remember that right?"

"Yes," said Holly. "Eternal Taiga is where Phoenix personnel came to 'in-process', or rather, to become official members of Phoenix. It was mostly about filling out paperwork, getting identification, getting fitted for uniforms, and receiving the equipment they needed to do their job."

"Phoenix. Yes. I remember. It was on the plaque up above, and back at the Barony."

"We can talk a little about that now," said Holly. "I'll be giving you a more thorough briefing later. But before I say more, please go get some food." She motioned to a nearby table. "I had the facility prepare a few items I thought you would enjoy."

"Oh my god," said Lin around a mouthful of food. "This is amazing. You have to try it, Countess! Uh...whatever it is."

"That is a cherry and cheese danish," said Holly. "The cheese is non-dairy, and the cherries are not exactly fresh. Not that you seemed to notice, judging by the speed in which you consumed it. It seems to have bypassed your mouth entirely!"

They all laughed hard. Countess went to prepare some food for herself. All of it looked amazing, like something the king and his court would eat at a ceremony. She selected several items at random and sat back down with the group.

Holly said, "Phoenix was a group of people who wanted to ensure that the government…like your kingdom…would survive a catastrophic event. A world-ending war, for example."

"Which is exactly what happened," said Vance.

"Yes," said Holly. "But Phoenix had been planning for this many years…decades prior. They built these facilities in secret with money that wasn't traceable, so no one would know or ask questions about them. When the war came, their underground empire was ready for them to escape into."

"How many other facilities are there?" asked Countess.

"Many," said Holly. "And most are still connected to each other via a large network of underground trains and roads."

"You're kidding," said Vance. "That's amazing!"

"It is amazing," said Holly. "A true technological marvel."

"If the Phoenix people escaped down here," said Lin. "I think it's natural to ask…where is everyone? This place seems abandoned. So did the place under the Barony."

"I don't know," said Holly. "I've never encountered anyone from Phoenix, and I've never read anything indicating that they ever came down here during or after the war. It's a mystery."

"Everything down here, it looks so new, like it was made yesterday," said Countess. "Yet, I know all of this is very old."

"These facilities are very old," said Holly. "And they use clever, invisible technology to keep themselves looking this way."

"How old?" asked Lin.

"This may surprise you. The war, what we call 'The Day of Fire', was over 700 years ago."

Countess's mouth fell open. "That's…how come we were never told about this?"

"I know about it," said Vance. He looked slightly proud of himself.

Countess looked at Lin. "Well, I can only speak for myself."

"No, I'm in the dark too," said Lin. "This has all been surprise after surprise to me."

"No need for you to know, I guess," said Holly. "I'm sure the Baron has his reasons. It's likely he didn't want to burden you."

As they finished eating, Countess couldn't help but feel a growing sense of apprehension. Holly's explanations were thorough, yet something about her calm demeanor seemed to hide more than it revealed. What else was she not telling them?

The team followed Holly down the hall to a room that said "Implantation" on a plaque next to the door.

"Now," said Holly. "The weapons I promised. This one is by far the most powerful. You may not agree at first, but after you've used it a while, you will understand."

"I don't get it," said Lin. "This looks like the same medical room that Vance got healed in."

"They are similar," said Holly, "but these beds are much more specialized. Not for healing."

"Implantation," said Countess. "What does it mean?"

"To put inside," said Holly.

Countess's eyes widened.

"Wait. Whoa, whoa, whoa," said Vance. "What...uh... Are you going to put something inside us?"

"Yes," said Holly, looking at him. "And I guarantee you're going to love it."

21

Countess emerged from unconsciousness into a strange sensory hell. She couldn't feel the right side of her body, and the parts she could feel on her left side burned like she was on fire.

"Taup"

Was someone saying something? She couldn't quite tell. Her vision was a blurry, red haze. Large black shadows swam in random directions across her field of view. She tried to scream, but all she heard was a low and distant drone.

"Top"

There it was again. Almost a human voice in a sea of static, distortion, and her own rapid heartbeat. Countess felt like she was falling backward endlessly. She shook her head from side to side. It didn't help. Her head felt large and heavy. She heard an impossibly high-pitched tone, followed by a loud hiss, which then tapered off. A muffled voice emerged from the auditory chaos.

"—tess!" It was Lin. "—Countess. Stop. Stop hitting me. I'm trying to help you!"

Countess shook her head again, then blinked her eyes furiously. Her vision swam. Lin's face was very close to hers, but something was off—his eyes weren't right. Not just wrong. Unfamiliar. Alien. What was wrong with him? She couldn't quite work it out. Suddenly she felt sick to her stomach.

"Guys…" Vance's voice came from her right. "Guys, I…I can't see." He sounded like he was crying. "Are you there? Please God…tell me you're there. Please…don't leave me like this!"

"Hey, hey…" said Lin in a soothing tone. "I'm with you."

Countess turned her head to the right. Her vision had large blurry blotches swimming around in it. Lin and Vance were kneeling nearby, facing each other. Vance's head was down, his chin almost touching his chest. A long trail of what looked like black ink streamed from his ear, leaving a trail down the side of his neck and onto his shoulder.

"It's okay, man. You're okay," said Lin. Then, in a louder voice, "Can you hear me?!"

Lin took his hands from Vance's shoulders and looked at them. They were shaking violently. Then, he fell over onto his side and began to convulse.

Countess saw a bright red mass at the corner of her vision. It was her own hand, and the palm was covered in blood. Her sight irised down to a small point, and then she heard a loud ringing.

The world went black, and she lost consciousness.

***

Countess wandered alone through the lower corridors of Eternal Taiga's medical level, restless. Her legs still ached from the implant procedure, and her mind hadn't stopped spinning since she'd awakened. Vance was sleeping. Lin was stable. Holly had encouraged her to rest.

But Countess didn't feel tired.

The facility's design was uniform, clinical—white hallways with glowing floor strips and quiet hisses from hidden ventilation. Most doors were labeled clearly: Recovery Suites, Triage, Diagnostics, and so on. But then she found a corridor she hadn't seen before.

It was colder here. The air had a sterile sharpness, like the inside of a sealed vial. And at the end of the hallway stood a heavy black door, flanked by small red status lights that blinked at irregular intervals.

On the center of the door, stamped in smooth gray metal, was a logo: a dark circular void surrounded by six sharp petals—stylized, symmetrical, and perfectly etched. It was austere, almost beautiful. Beneath the symbol were five stark letters:

ASPHODEL

Countess stared at it. Something about the design bothered her— not because she understood it, but because it felt ancient in a way that technology wasn't supposed to. Like a warning dressed up as a flower.

She stepped closer, and the lights on either side of the door clicked yellow, then green.

"Access granted," a female voice whispered from the wall panel.

Countess hesitated.

The door didn't open—but something behind her did.

She turned.

Holly stood in the middle of the hallway, bathed in soft white light from the ceiling above. Her small form was still—a childlike shadow cast far too long—and her eyes glowed a cold, perfect blue.

"Don't go in there," she said.

Countess blinked. Holly hadn't appeared with the usual shimmer or soft chime. She was just... there. Silent. Watching.

"What is this place?" Countess asked, already knowing she wouldn't get a straight answer.

"You're not ready to know."

Countess gestured toward the door. "It let me in."

"That was an oversight on my part."

The blue glow intensified, refracting faintly across the white walls, and casting fractured halos across the floor.

"What's inside?" Countess asked.

Holly took a single step forward. "Seeing what's inside would only upset you."

Countess swallowed, her fingers brushing the grip of her weapon out of instinct. She wasn't afraid of Holly—not exactly—but something about this version of her, this still and solemn guardian posture, was... wrong.

"Are there...people in there?"

"No," Holly said softly. "There are souls."

The word hit her like a punch.

Countess took a step back from the door. Holly's eyes dimmed slightly, sensing her retreat.

"You're not ready," she repeated. "But one day... you will be. All must be revealed at the right time, in the right order."

And without another word, Holly vanished—her soligram flickering out like a breath on glass.

The hallway lights returned to their normal hue.

The ASPHODEL door lights blinked red.

Access denied.

Countess turned away and walked back toward the main medical hallway. She didn't look back.

But she couldn't stop thinking about the symbol. Or the word.

Not "people."

Not "patients."

Souls.

22

Countess opened her eyes, but the room was a blur. She felt better, but there was a lingering grogginess from the anesthetic.

"How long has it been?" asked Lin, his voice hoarse and strained.

"Thirty hours, give or take," said Holly. "The beds finished the process, but there was an implantation error. It kicked you out halfway through, causing severe strain on your system. A good thing, as it turns out. You could have died in there. Lin, I appreciate that you were able to help the others, despite your difficulties."

"You could have fucking warned us!" Lin's voice rose in frustration. His fists clenched at his sides.

"I'm sorry," Holly said, genuine sympathy in her eyes. "This equipment is very old, and there's nobody to maintain or calibrate it. It doesn't always happen, but it is a risk. And personally, I believe the reward is worth the risk."

Countess heard real sympathy in Holly's voice and appreciated it. Just when she thought Holly was hiding an evil side, kind words such as these shined through.

"Always?" Vance interjected. "So you've done this before? There were others?"

"Many others," Holly replied.

"Wait," said Lin. "Where are they? What happened to them all?"

"I help the Baron," said Holly. She sounded defensive. "I give people what they need and see that they get to where they need to go. After that, it's not my problem."

"Great," Lin muttered. "This is just fucking great."

Countess turned onto her side, which took more effort than she expected. "So," she said. "We survived your implantation process.

Now what?"

"Now," said Holly, "you get to see what your suffering has earned you."

"I fucking hope so!" Lin exclaimed. "Because aside from breakfast, this whole business has been a shit show."

"He's not wrong," Countess agreed. "And speaking of food…"

"Hey, yeah," Vance chimed in, "I'm starving!"

"Of course," Holly said.

After a tense silence, they all moved to the dining hall, where Holly prepared a wonderful meal for them.

***

"I'm not so sure," said Countess. "It's a lot. It's been a lot to take in." She looked down at her hands, which still shook slightly. She clenched them into fists and set them down on the table. Countess was struggling. She needed to be strong for her team, but had never felt weaker, afraid, and exposed. Each breath felt like a test of her resolve, but she couldn't afford to falter now. She exhaled long and steady, a calming technique she'd learned in the intelligence service. It worked somewhat, lessening the trembling in her hands.

They were all seated in the dining hall, and Holly was standing on top of the table near Countess. Lin and Vance were at another table nearby, talking excitedly and shoveling food into their faces.

"I understand," said Holly. "You and your team have been through a lot. But let me show you what you've gained, by way of a demonstration."

"Fair enough—" said Countess. But she didn't finish. As she spoke, Holly disappeared.

"What?" Countess stood up from the table and took a step back. "What the hell?!"

"You see," Holly's voice continued. "I've been down on one of the training levels since you went back into the implantation beds. Look down."

Countess bent over slightly and gasped. The floor turned transparent, and part of the building's structural members, electrical wiring, and ductwork was revealed. Through it all, about a hundred feet down, a little figure waved. The view zoomed, and Holly became much bigger. She waved again.

"Here I am!" said Holly. The floor became opaque, and Holly reappeared on top of the table. Then, there were three of Holly. One crossed her arms, another saluted, and the third gave an emphatic double-thumbs-up.

"Whoa!" said Vance. "This is amazing!"

"One of the things the Typhon implant does is allow for graphical overlays onto your vision."

"What...what the hell does that mean?" said Lin. He felt like he spoke too loud. There was something off about his hearing. When others spoke, there was a loud hissing. It hurt him, like someone was driving an icepick into his eardrum.

Countess passed her hand through one Holly.

"So this isn't...real?" asked Countess. "You aren't real?" Two of the Hollys disappeared, leaving just one.

"It's a projection. A party trick. Think of it like a small picture of me being pinned up inside your eyes. You see the world around you, but the image of me is in front. That's a very simplified explanation, of course, but hopefully, you get the point. And this overlay...it barely scratches the surface of what Typhon can do. Sounds can be projected as well."

"Show us," said Countess. She sat back down.

A crude and sexless representation of a human body appeared to hover over the table in a T-pose. It sunk into the table until just the head and neck were at Countess's eye level. The head turned transparent and began to slowly rotate. Bright red points of light appeared at several locations inside the head.

"The implantation process affected many sites within your bodies, mostly inside your brains."

"How?" said Lin. "I don't see any wounds on our heads. You're saying machines were digging around in our skulls?" Lin was having trouble concentrating. The images Holly showed were all over-saturated and blown-out, like walking out into bright sunlight after being in the dark for a long time.

Countess noticed a sharp sound to Lin's voice. She looked at him and saw that he was sweating.

"Lin," she said, "are you alright?"

"Uh, yeah," said Lin. "Fine." But she could tell he wasn't fine. He put his hands on the side of his head, closed his eyes, and rubbed his temples. Countess watched this, concerned.

"The process is more elegant than that," said Holly. "Teams of tiny machines floated through your blood vessels and worked in coordination to build structures inside your bodies. It's called nanotechnology. Very powerful."

Countess struggled to understand the technical terms, feeling a step behind the rapid explanations. She could tell that Vance understood what he was seeing and hearing, so she decided that she'd follow up with him later for any clarification.

The view zoomed in to one of the dots, and swarms of what looked like insects moved and assembled complex, three-dimensional structures more complex than anything Countess had ever seen.

"I've trained on a lot of advanced stuff in my time," said Vance. "At least...I thought it was advanced at the time. I had no idea this level of tech was even possible!" Countess had never seen Vance so excited. She was actually happy for him. Her mind snapped back to Lin. He might be in trouble. Holly sounded like she was on a roll, so Countess let her continue.

"The Typhon implant, the technology you now have in your bodies, was state-of-the-art before the war," said Holly. "Ninety-nine percent of the population had no idea it even existed. Think of it as very secret military technology...which it is. Phoenix didn't create it, but they did use it effectively."

The human head disappeared and was replaced by a technical-looking diagram. It faded, and another appeared in its place. Then another.

"Design, engineering, and maintenance were all areas that benefited from this technology," said Holly. "For example..."

The diagram shifted and zoomed to a large component in the system. A man's voice narrated text that appeared beside it.

"The Keplar Industrial KCM Chill-Max turbine provides rapid expansion of bleed air taken from the reactor..."

The diagram was replaced by another. The schematic shifted, and a component was isolated. It brightened while the rest of the diagram dimmed. This time, a female voice narrated.

"Vorpal Industries VPL506G busway is an excellent choice for any demanding, large-scale facility. The two-inch copper bus duct provides 600 amps—"

The diagram disappeared.

"Are we supposed to understand any of that?" said Countess.

"Those were two annotated system diagrams that describe how the technology hidden in the walls around you works," said Holly. "Here's something you'll find more familiar."

A still image appeared. It was the security checkpoint they had passed through before they came down to this level. Several men in sophisticated-looking camouflage uniforms stood behind the transparent walls. Countess was having trouble understanding what she was seeing. The men had intricately-crafted, matte-black tools of some kind in their hands, which they were aiming into the horizontal slits in the walls.

"Those are guns, right?" said Vance.

Lin said, "Gun? What's a gun?" He wiped his brow. He met Countess's gaze for a moment, then looked away. Lin's heart pounded in his chest, each beat echoing in his ears. He wasn't right. His body was failing all around him, and he felt trapped inside.

"Holly—" said Countess, but Holly ignored her.

"We'll be getting into ballistics as part of your training," said Holly. "But I suppose it won't hurt to get a primer."

The view zoomed in on one of the guns. A deep male voice narrated.

"The Heckler & Koch MP7A2 is a next-generation, enhanced-performance firearm that bridges the gap between assault rifles and conventional submachine guns. Developed as a personal defense weapon, it far exceeds the NATO requirements for defeating cheap and effective soft body armor..."

The image disappeared, and the voice cut off.

A video played of a man in a different camouflage uniform. He was wearing angular, transparent eyewear and held a gun tightly to his shoulder. It bucked in his hands, and to Countess's ears, gave off a sound like a spoon rapidly tapping a metal table. The scene was replaced by a paper target with the outline of a human torso. Several small holes were punched into the target in rapid succession.

"I…I don't," said Lin. His voice was trembling. "I don't understand any of this!" He stood up from the table and ran a forearm across his drenched brow.

Lin was now covered in sweat, and his eyes were wide.

"Too much, too much," said Lin. "I…this isn't me. I…I need to get out of here." He was now backing into a corner.

"Hey, hey…whoa there," said Countess in as soothing a voice as she could manage. "Lin…It's going to be okay." She reached out to put her hand on his arm, but he recoiled.

"Don't touch me!" Lin looked like a caged animal. "I don't know what's happening to me." He looked from person to person, like they were going to pounce on him at any moment. Then he looked down at his own hands. A look of horror flashed across his face, as if he couldn't believe what he was seeing.

"Holly…" said Countess. "Can you disable Lin's implants?"

"Yes, but—"

"Do it."

Lin looked up in horror, then collapsed. Countess was at his side checking his vital signs. He was unconscious. Alive, but breathing shallow and rapid. Countess looked to Holly, who seemed like she was reading something.

"Will he be ok?!"

"He'll be fine," said Holly. "I'm just looking at his calibration settings and they are way out of whack."

"What does that mean?" said Countess.

"Poor Lin was suffering from sensory overload," said Holly. She seemed sad. "I can only imagine what he must have been experiencing. Lights too bright. Sounds too loud. Lin's pain receptors were being interpreted as ambient noise. That's why everything hurt."

"Can you fix him?" said Vance. He sounded more desperate than he intended.

"Yes," said Holly. "I'll work on this now."

Sometime later, Countess sat across from Lin and Vance. They had found some comfortable chairs in a small office nearby. Countess asked Holly for some private time, and she agreed.

Lin was looking much more composed now, but Countess could tell he would need some more time to himself.

"God, that was fucking awful," he said. "Once we turned down the brightness... the sound... She said it was a calibration issue, whatever the fuck that is."

"Wow," said Vance. "I can see why you were overwhelmed. Not cool. I would have been climbing the walls." Vance smiled at Lin. "But I'm glad you're still with us, buddy."

"Fuck off," said Lin. They both laughed, but the mirth was only half-felt.

"Yeah," said Countess. "This is yet another failure that has been out of our control. And we've all just had to... deal with it." She looked away and shook her head.

"I want you to know that I'm proud of you both. Ever since we left Yorke, it's been mayhem. Mayhem non-stop."

"Yeah, it has," said Lin. "Listen Countess, I'm sorry I—"

"No," said Countess. "Don't." She looked at them both seriously. "Our kingdom has asked a lot of us over the years. What happened to us over the past couple of days would challenge anyone. Neither of you did anything wrong. And you certainly have nothing to be ashamed of. I appreciate how both of you have conducted yourselves."

"So, this is what the Baron sent us here for?" said Lin. "This... Typhon thing?"

"It's amazing," said Vance, then he considered Lin. "I mean, I know you're... probably hating it right now, but, I mean... I've trained on some high-tech equipment before, but this!"

"Yes, it's military-grade hardware and software," said Countess. "Holly says we need it. Apparently, the Phoenix people, the ones that built all this..." She made a sweeping motion, indicating the facility around them. "...they used the implant to help them do their daily work. It's a tool. People could talk to one another from far away, show each other what they were working on, and conduct meetings when everyone was in different places."

"Or read a manual on how to fix or build something," said Vance, "without carrying books around. It's a total game-changer!" Vance looked like his eyes were going to pop out of his head. "Sorry. I get a little excited by technology. And this is the best, most advanced I've ever seen. I'm dedicating my life to this! I need to learn everything!"

"You're using a lot of terms I don't know or understand," said Lin, "but I get it. It's powerful, and it can help us work better together. That's all I need to know."

"Exactly," said Countess. "And that's what we need to do—work together. I saw the carnage the pagans left behind at Greystone Barony. They have weapons that can cook a person inside a suit of armor, and without even damaging the armor itself."

Vance's eyes went wide. "Seriously?"

"Yes," said Countess, "so we need everything we can get to stop them. Holly wants us to start training right away, but I said we need rest first, so we'll start fresh in the morning. Are you both okay with that?"

"Yeah," said Vance. "I Can't wait to see what this tech can do!"

"Lin?" Countess looked at him, but he was looking at the floor. He exhaled forcefully. "Yeah. Yeah, let's do this."

He met Countess's eyes. She nodded with a smile, glad to see he was still willing to continue.

"The downtime will do me good," said Lin. "I'll be ready to go in the morning."

"Good," said Countess. "I wish I could say 'if you need something, just ask,' but I honestly don't have anything to give." She stood. "We're all in this together, and my expectation is that we work together to see this through."

Lin and Vance stood, then both nodded.

"Get some rest," said Countess. She shifted her gaze from Vance to Lin. "And if you want to speak with me privately, I'm available."

Countess walked outside and sat by herself. She thought of recent events and how hard things had been for them all. Not in a self-defeating way, but in a kind of satisfied amazement. Lin and Vance were so resilient. Despite the pain and confusion, they had persevered. Countess felt a renewed sense of purpose. They had faced setbacks, but they were stronger together. Tomorrow would bring new challenges, but tonight, they would rest and prepare.

They were both still standing. That was enough for now. The cost would come later.

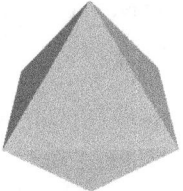

23

All the hostages were killed, mowed down by terrorist gunfire, and Holly stopped the training simulation. Lin threw his helmet down so hard it bounced over his head.

"God fucking damn it!"

Vance lay down on the floor, sighed hard, and put his hands over his face. Countess bent over, placing her hands on her knees to catch her breath. She felt like spitting. They'd been training hard for two days, and the team was getting tired and frustrated.

Countess' team trained in the largest available room, which was enormous. Countess was certain that all of Cushing Cottage, including the towers and outer wall, would fit inside. The room was empty, colored light gray, and lacked any decoration or function. All the magic was performed by their Typhon implants.

Holly supervised their training from an elevated booth overlooking the training room. The entire wall facing the inside of the room was made of non-reflective glass, and Holly could be seen pacing back and forth inside.

"I told you to keep up!" Lin snapped at Vance. "You were late on the entry and we lost the initiative."

"I went in as fast as I could," Vance replied, exasperated. "There were just too many. Couldn't take 'em down fast enough."

"Stop it, you two," Countess interjected. "It wasn't an entry problem. The plan wasn't good enough. I—"

"Enough," Holly said. Her face appeared as a small talking head in the lower right corner of their heads-up display. "This is no time for bickering. You go again."

Holly paused for a moment. She knew the team was approaching exhaustion, so she decided to give them some words of wisdom before shoving them back into the simulation.

"Work together," Holly said. "Think. Pay close attention to your surroundings and what resources you have available. You can do this."

The team looked up at her, and they all nodded, but less enthusiastically than she would have liked.

"Can't we run the same one again, at least?" Vance asked. "That way, we can plan for—"

"No," Holly cut him off. "That's not how this works. These are randomized, drop-in scenarios. Just do the best you can with what you have."

"Okay, let's run it again. Get into position!"

Countess, Lin, and Vance lined up, shoulder to shoulder, and clasped their hands in front of them. They were all wearing dark-gray coveralls, light body armor, and non-functional sub-machine guns and sidearms. Their main weapons hung down from complex upper-body harnesses, which had a dizzying array of pouches and slots for ammo of all kinds. The simulation would fill these, as required by the scenario.

"Ready, ready," Holly said. "Go, go, go."

On the last "Go," Countess' world changed. They were all inside a vehicle that was moving through the air over a large body of water. Countess felt a wave of vertigo as she looked around. They were all seated, wearing dark-blue and gray camouflage, and lightweight body armor. The simulated apparel was much fancier and well-designed than what they were actually wearing.

The roar of the twin rotors thundered overhead, vibrating through their seats and into their bones. Wind knifed through the open doors, whipping hair and loose straps like angry snakes. The cabin was deafening—rotor thrum, garbled comms chatter, and the high-pitched whine of turbines merging into a single oppressive noise. Countess had to focus just to breathe normally.

"Helicopter," Vance said. "Or chopper, if you prefer." His voice sounded high-pitched and had an odd quality, like he was talking through a long tube. Countess realized they were all wearing what looked like plastic cups on their ears—communication headsets, as they were called in the briefings. They also wore sophisticated, eye-protection glasses. Countess didn't see why they were needed at first. But after a few missions, it became obvious. Airborne debris was constantly flying around during the final moments—from wood splinters to actual bullets. The impact-resistant glasses couldn't stop a bullet directly, but they could save an eye from a ricochet.

"UH-60 Blackhawk," Vance continued. "A common troop transport for missions like this back before the Day of Fire."

"Not important," Lin said.

"Leave him alone," Countess said. "The additional intel is helpful. Thank you, Vance."

They were descending toward a chaotic war-zone. Several large ships were on fire, and at least two were capsized and in the process of sinking. They all surrounded some kind of multi-platform structure.

Countess felt several thumps, like someone was tapping on the side of their aircraft with a metal hammer. The helicopter moved sideways, and Countess's stomach felt like it was left behind.

"We're taking small arms fire from one of the ships below," Vance said.

There was a loud hissing sound. The sound repeated three more times, then an explosion below. The helicopter shook violently.

"What the fuck was that?" Lin shouted.

"Ghostrider," Vance replied. "AC-130. Gunship."

"No idea what you just said," Lin said.

"It's an aircraft, like we're flying in. But it's got a lot of guns sticking out of the side. It's on our side. Providing air support so we can land on the platform down there." Vance pointed emphatically.

A few moments later, Vance said, "Brace yourselves. Pilot says this is gonna be a combat landing." Countess grabbed a handful of the red, mesh seat-back behind her. It didn't help.

The helicopter landed so hard Countess felt her teeth rattle. The craft slid sideways several feet, its engines whining. The pilot fought with the controls as the aircraft bucked side-to-side, threatening to flip over. The wrestling match was won, and the angry machine came to rest.

As soon as the helicopter stopped moving, Countess, Lin, and Vance were out. They half-jogged, hunched over, toward a plume of green smoke. A man in dark goggles waved them over.

The chopper lifted off and turned to leave, but it was struck by something large and fast. The aircraft exploded in a large fireball. The heat of it burned Countess's skin, and the shock-wave knocked her down.

Lin was hit by a piece of flaming debris and blown sideways. Vance was on him instantly, removing the flaming part and patting out the flames.

"Get the fuck off me!" Lin batted Vance out of the way, struggled to his knees, and clawed the partially melted glasses off his face. "FUCK!"

Countess ran to him and helped him to his feet.

"What happened?" Countess asked.

"Missile shot down the chopper," Vance said. "Looks like we got out just in time."

Countess' eyes were wide. Only a few minutes in, and this mission was more intense than anything she'd experienced in her intelligence career.

"Is that it?" Lin asked. "I mean, was that the mission?"

Countess looked around, taking in the situation. "I don't think so. That guy over there is trying to get our attention." The man by the green smoke was still waving.

"Anyone injured?" Countess asked.

"Just my ego," Lin said.

"Okay, let's go."

They ran over to the man wearing goggles. On the wall, there was a metal sign. Black letters on a beige background announced: "Joint Base Tiberius." Goggles pointed to another man nearby, who was gesturing emphatically to two people in front of him. As Countess's team approached, the two peeled off and ran down some nearby stairs, out of sight.

"There you are!" said the man. "I'm glad you got here in one piece. Thanks for coming on such short notice."

Bright, orange text appeared on Countess' heads-up display. They were lines she was supposed to say.

"Uh, we were in the area," Countess said. She started rough but eased into it. "Consular protection duty in Mumbai. Sorry there aren't more of us. Rest of the team is back in Norfolk."

"Happy to have you," said the man. "I heard what you guys did in Sarajevo back in '19. Fucking legendary. I'm Tim Scott, 24th STS."

Countess shook his hand and looked at the rank on his shoulder. A white line extended from the insignia, and helpful text was added: "Major, United States Air Force." The Typhon implant made suggestions like this when Countess' eyes came to rest on something it found interesting.

"It's good to meet you, Major," she said. "What's the situation?"

Tim took two steps back, and the space between them was suddenly filled with a rotating three-dimensional engineering blueprint of the platform complex.

"Thirty-nine hostages. All being held here."

The blueprint stopped rotating and zoomed in on a large structure high above one of the platforms.

"This is Aerostat Dominus," said the Major. "It's a large Surveillance aircraft. I know what you're thinking, but don't worry. We'll fly you up there."

The blueprint zoomed again. Inside the aerostat was an industrial area, three enormous mesh parts baskets were hanging over large pools of bubbling, glowing green liquid. Ten or more people were in each basket.

"The hostages are suspended over three large vats of solvent. If they fall in there... dead in 10 seconds."

"Are you fucking kidding me?" Lin exclaimed.

The Major ignored him. "Drone got this footage about twenty minutes ago."

A video played on the team's heads-up display. The drone emerged from a hole in the wall and flew into a large open area. Sunlight entered through the roof, which was transparent and comprised of rows of horizontal windows.

The scene showed three levels: the ground level with the three chemical vats, the level above with walkways and balconies overlooking the work area below, and about 25 feet above, a maze of slender catwalks. Men with rifles were on all of these levels.

"OPFOR count is twenty-five. Russian. Most of them Wagner Group. Hired muscle. But their command structure is Vympel. That's why we called you in. Your counter-terrorism experience will be vital in this situation."

Purple text appeared on her HUD. Vance: "Wagner Group are Russian mercenaries, a fair threat. But the Vympel are a top-tier unit of the Spetsnaz. FSB. They are lethal. Extremely well-trained and equipped." (Sorry, I didn't mean to throw a lot of strange terms at you!)

"One moment," said Countess. She thought about what she had just heard. It sounded like a recipe for disaster, just like the last mission. There were too many terrorists, and her team wasn't big enough. If they rushed in there, all of the hostages were going to be killed.

"Who's available for tasking?" Countess asked.

"I have a team of six," said the Major. "There's a SEAL team in a Zodiac patrolling the area around the platforms. They can be recalled in an emergency. But otherwise, I don't want to pull them from their duty."

He thought for a moment, then added, "Oh, and there's a small team of Australian SASR guys over there."

Countess looked at the men and winced. They were just about the sorriest thing she'd ever seen. They were dirty, unshaven, and all had dark bags under their eyes.

"They're just here as observers," the Major continued, "but you might convince them to help. Just know…they're in from Malaysia. Some kind of long recon thing. They're probably not in the best of moods. If you go that route, my recommendation is to tread lightly. No one's on their best behavior when they're tired and hungry."

"Understood," said Countess.

More purple text from Vance. Vance: "SASR: Special Air Service Regiment. Australia's premier army counter-terrorist unit. Respected by many as one of the best fighting forces in the world."

Countess wrote back: "These guys? They don't look it."

Yellow text from Lin: "Don't judge a book by its cover."

Countess ran over to the small Australian team. "I need you."

"Fair Dinkum," said one, stepping forward.

"Don't say that shit," said another. "They'll think we actually talk like that."

The first man had a wry smile on his face. "Just giving the Yanks a show."

"And by show, you mean making them think we're a bunch of cartoon characters. Shut the fuck up."

The first one laughed, then looked Countess in the eyes. "Right. Now how can we help, madam?"

Countess considered them all for a few seconds, then sighed. "When was the last time you had something to eat?"

The man nodded. "It's been a while."

She fished around in her pockets and pulled out an energy bar. "You two," she said to her team. "Any food you have, give it up." Three more bars were produced, and Countess handed them to the man.

The man handed the bars out to his team, retaining one for himself.

"I don't know who you are, or what you need," said the man, tearing off the energy bar's wrapper. "But for this... we'll follow you into the flames of Tartarus."

They all laughed.

"I'm Finn," said the man. "Finn McDuff."

Countess shook the man's hand. "It's good to meet you, Finn. Let me tell you my plan."

***

"Do you have any rope and breaching charges?" Finn asked.

"Yep," said the Major. "Talk to my man there. He'll get you set up."

The Major held up his hand for the Australians and his own men to see. "Five minutes. Be back here and ready to go." The Australians departed.

The Major looked down his nose at Countess like he was a schoolmaster. "You work with these guys before?"

"No," said Countess.

"That's pretty risky, all things considered."

"I have a good sense about people," said Countess. "And besides, it's not as risky as what I'm about to ask you and your men to do."

***

Countess gave the order to breach, and there were three explosions overhead. The door next to her disintegrated, blown to pieces by a more-than-adequate breaching charge. Countess entered the doorway and began shooting Vympel operators.

Glass rained down on Countess from above, glancing off her helmet and shoulders with little popping sounds. Five flash-bangs went off like a pack of industrial firecrackers. The Typhon implants reacted with super-human speed, sparing the team's vision and hearing.

Above, the Australians were dropping in, headfirst, through the skylights. They were being lowered on ropes, which were clasped between their legs. Each had a pistol in both hands, and they were firing down onto some very surprised Russians.

One floor above, the Major's team was eliminating the Wagner Group hustle.

The Vympel leader ran for the basket release handles, and Countess put two bullets into his temple. He fell forward onto the handles, his dead weight actuating them.

The baskets hurtled down toward the boiling vats of solvent, and the hostages inside screamed like banshees. Countess body-checked the terrorist leader off the levers, and quickly reset the first one. But when she grabbed the second, she lost her footing, slipping in a pool of blood. The second lever was pulled back by the momentum of her falling weight, but now Countess was flailing on the ground. She watched helplessly, as the third basket finished its travel home.

The bottom of the third basket crashed into the solvent but did not enter. A large gout of the toxic liquid was sent in all directions. Thankfully, it didn't land on anything or anyone important.

Confused, Countess looked up at the third lever's handle. There was a hand on it. And the hand was attached to Lin. He looked down at her with a big grin.

"Need a hand?"

"Yes, actually," she said.

Countess got to her feet, and there was a strange noise all around her. Applause.

She looked up. The Major and his 24th STS team were all looking down, clapping. Above them, on the catwalks, the Australian SASR were all grinning. Finn gave a two-fingered salute, then put his hands to the sides of his mouth and yelled, "Good job, Yanks."

The world around Countess dissolved, and the flat, gray walls of the training room returned. And in that moment, she felt really proud.

"Mission accomplished," said Holly. "Lin and Vance, you're dismissed. Dinner should be ready when you get to the dining hall. Countess, would you stay behind, please?"

Countess noticed there was a strange quality to Holly's voice. She seemed upset.

***

"Everything okay?" Countess asked. She was sitting on a comfortable chair in the control booth, looking out into the training room.

Holly ignored the question and asked one of her own. "How do you think the team's progressing?"

"I think they're doing well, but I have some concerns," said Countess. "Lin can be arrogant and overbearing. He's been better since the incident. Vance is coming out of his shell, offering good information when needed, but he's still meek in some high-stress situations."

Holly was nodding at Countess' observations. She seemed to be deep in thought.

"Overall," said Countess. "I'm proud to be serving with them. I don't know what to expect with this Priestess Vilma character, but... I promise we'll do our best. Yeah. With these new weapons and Typhon, we might just pull this off."

Holly considered Countess for several long moments. "Agreed." Then she looked away. "Countess, I want you to know something. And I'm struggling with this, because my job requires me to keep an emotional distance from you."

"But—"

"No, let me finish. You see… these missions… the ones I put your team through today… they aren't meant to be won. In fact, they're purpose-built to be unwinnable. Phoenix nicknamed them 'Kobayashi Maru,' kept them in a folder with that name."

"I don't—"

"Please," said Holly. She collected herself. "But you did it. Your team completed the mission, saved the hostages. All of them. It's unbelievable, and I've never seen anything like it. To my knowledge, no one has ever beaten one of these missions."

Holly sighed, thought for a moment, then continued. "I record all of these missions. It's just part of my work." She smiled. "I just know I'm going to be replaying this one over and over for my own enjoyment."

Holly looked at Countess, her stare intense. "When you say 'you just might pull this off,' I think you're right. And not just against Priestess and her team, but I think you're right in a way you don't understand yet."

"I appreciate what you're saying," said Countess. "Maybe I don't understand all of your words, but I know you're paying me a compliment. So, thank you."

"Go join your team at dinner," said Holly, "and get a good night's sleep. Because tomorrow, you're gonna need it."

24

Countess went to breakfast in full tactical gear, expecting another grueling day of simulations. But something had changed. Lin and Vance were in a cheerful mood, and Holly actually smiled at her when she arrived.

"No training today!" Vance said, as happy as she had ever seen him. Countess felt a sense of relief wash over her. The past few days were brutal, and last night she went to bed completely drained.

Lin and Vance were already seated and eating when Countess arrived. Holly was sitting in the middle of the round table, as she normally did. Countess filled a plate with food and sat down close to Holly. She reached out and grabbed Holly's arm.

"Hey!" said Holly. "Boundaries!" She had a hurt look on her face.

Countess laughed. "I was just checking to see if you were really there."

"Yes, I'm here. And I'm glad you all are, too. I have something important to share."

"Briefing," Lin and Vance said simultaneously. The word hung in the air over Holly's head in large, block letters. Countess took her plate and sat next to Lin and Vance.

"Countess, you and your team have done really well the past two days," said Holly. "I wish we could spend more time training, but we can't. This was picked up a little while ago at a facility north of here."

A gray-scale picture of three pagans leaving a low building appeared.

"The plan was to have you intercept the pagans before they reached the facility, but they are proving to be a lot more resourceful than expected."

A map of the region appeared, more accurate than any map she had seen of the two kingdoms.

"We are here," said Holly, placing a yellow circle near Poughkeepsie. Then the map shifted north.

"What is ALL Banny?" said Lin. "Never heard of it."

"Albany," said Holly, correcting Lin. "It used to be the capital of New York before the war. There's not much there now. At least, on the surface."

"I know New York," said Lin. "That's what they called this land in ancient times."

"Before the Day of Fire," said Vance.

Holly looked impatient. "Right," she said, "The pagans were detected exiting a train. Here." Another yellow marker was placed on the map. Then the photo of the pagans returned.

"Ah," said Countess. "So that's what a train looks like."

Several more images were displayed, close-ups of each of the pagans' faces. The last was a dark-skinned woman with long, braided hair adorned with small ornaments.

"Whoa," said Vance. "She's beautiful."

"Settle down there, lover boy," said Lin. "She's the enemy, remember?"

Vance frowned.

"This is Priestess Vilma," said Holly. "Or, simply…'Priestess'. That's what her team calls her."

"What are they doing there? What is this place?" said Lin.

"I'm getting to that," said Holly. "The facility is a lab complex specializing in experimental nanotechnology. I don't have time to go into details, but some of the systems in your implants were developed there."

"Cool," said Vance.

"The facility's called Aether Storm."

Countess mouthed the name without saying it out loud.

"Most of Aether Storm is support for the labs, which are in a large open area on the east side of the complex."

A plan view of the Aether Storm complex appeared above Holly. To Countess, it looked like a really complicated blueprint. There were lots of small details she didn't quite understand. The view shifted, zooming in on an area of many concentric circles.

"They're going for the lab building here," continued Holly, "which is where the other Ring of Callifrey is stored."

"Priestess and her team must be stopped before they can acquire the ring. I thought we had more time, but apparently they discovered the location and are going straight for it."

"So, we have to go right away!" said Countess.

"Yeah, what are we waiting for?" said Lin.

"We have a little time yet," said Holly. "The labs have excellent security. Even a security expert like Vance would have a serious challenge getting through it. So finish eating, get your gear in order, and meet back here in thirty minutes."

Holly looked at each of them seriously. "One more thing. If they get into the labs and you have to go in after them, I can't go with you. This... Gumdrop," Holly indicated herself, "...won't work in there. There's too much interference."

"Duly noted," said Countess.

"Any questions?" asked Holly. There were none.

"Remember," she said. "The Typhon implant is a tool. It can be subverted, so don't completely trust it or lean on it. You can, however, trust your teammates. They are your most valuable resource. Thank you. That is all."

***

Lin and Vance had been reduced to little boys, whooping and laughing about how excited they were to be going so fast. The train was amazing. Countess was amazed herself. The accommodations were fancier than a king's coach. Everything was bright, smooth, polished, and well-lit. The seats were heaven; easily the most comfortable she'd ever sat on. They were made out of a material that seemed to move around on its own, forming a close bond to her body. The effect was so relaxing she thought about taking a nap.

Holly's voice came over the implant. She was on the train, but not in the same section. "The facility is about 135 kilometers. It should take about 30 minutes to get there. I'll give you some privacy. I won't bother you again until we get there."

Lin and Vance came and sat across from Countess.

Countess yawned. "You should both be going over Holly's briefing, or catching a quick nap. I don't care which." She smiled and looked outside. "Napping is what I plan to do."

"We need to talk," said Lin. His voice was almost a whisper, and he had an intense look on his face. "It's important."

"Ok..." said Countess. She gave them both an expectant look.

"It's the beds," said Lance. "The ones that gave us these Typhon implants."

"So? What about them?" she said.

"They couldn't have done it."

"What?" said Countess. "How do you figure that?"

"They're for Cesarean operations," said Lin. Vance nodded.

"Ok. Let me get this straight. You're saying that the beds that Holly put us in...were made to pull babies out of pregnant women?"

"Yes, they only have that function," said Vance. "And there's something else. They're all broken."

"What? No. That can't be right," said Countess.

"It's true," said Lin. "Vance showed me. We looked at the beds, the schematics, and the diagnostics data. They haven't worked for hundreds of years."

Countess was confused. "What does this mean?"

"It means," said Lin, "that when we came into that facility back there...we already had the Typhon implants inside us."

"Had to," said Vance. "I think we've always had it."

"And by always," said Countess, "you mean—"

"It's true," said Holly. She startled them all by appearing in the aisle nearby. "I guess there's no use in hiding it. You've had the technology inside you since you were born."

Countess remembered being ten years old, outrunning her entire regiment during a training exercise. The instructors said it was talent. Now she wasn't so sure.

Countess's eyes went wide. "Wha... Hey. You said you were giving us privacy!"

"I lied," said Holly.

"It seems like you've lied to us about a lot of things," said Lin.

"More than you know," said Holly. "More by omission, than anything else."

Countess looked hurt. "I don't understand. Why—"

"You're in the middle of something big and important. You're all in the intelligence business. You have been for a long time. You know that operational security is required. And sometimes, even people who are in the middle of things must be kept in the dark. Right?"

Countess looked at Lin and Vance. "Well, yes, that's true, but—"

"What's true," said Holly," is that each of you is very special. I wish I could tell you how special. A lot of work has gone into making you as good as you are. And I'm not talking about your intelligence training and experience."

"What else aren't you telling us?" asked Vance. He looked disappointed.

"Quite a lot, actually," said Holly, "but here's what you need to know…what you already know: Yorke Kingdom needs your help. You now have the tools and the training to accomplish your mission."

Countess hated how betrayed she felt—and hated even more the part of her that still wanted to believe Holly.

Holly pointed in the direction the train was heading. "Priestess has possession of part of a weapon of mass destruction. If she gets the other half, she could destroy Yorke Kingdom. Everyone and everything you've ever known…gone in an instant. This is the most serious threat the kingdom has ever faced."

Holly pointed at herself. "I've done my part—followed the Baron's orders. Now it's time for you to do your part. You have an opportunity to be heroes for the kingdom—don't let her down."

"We take our oath to Yorke Kingdom seriously," said Countess. "We wouldn't have come this far if we didn't. But when are you going to tell us what's really going on here?"

"I want to tell you," said Holly. "It depends on the outcome of this mission. Simple as that."

Lin crossed his arms. "This is all bullshit."

Holly raised her eyebrows. "You're right. It is."

ACT III - AETHER STORM

25

They were ready to kill on sight.

The train doors hissed open, and Countess' team swept out as one—silent, precise, lethal. Clad in dark tactical armor and equipped with submachine guns, grenades, and HUD-linked optics, they moved like spirits of vengeance summoned to sacred ground.

Orders: Move to Contact, their display read.

They entered the arrival hall of Aether Storm.

Aether Storm didn't look like a military facility. It didn't look like anything Countess had ever seen. The station was luminous, the polished floor etched with gold-inlaid sacred geometry—concentric rings, triangles, spirals, and the unmistakable form of a dodecahedron. Gilded statues lined the colonnades, each depicting solemn figures with halos of data-filaments, offering tools like relics: circuit boards, crystalline blades, surgical implements. A stained diamond canopy arched high overhead, casting rainbow motes through the steam and nanomist that drifted across the tiles.

"Train Station," said Holly, appearing as a miniature soligram on Countess's shoulder. She was dressed like a medieval abbess now. Her tiny dark robe was unadorned, but she wore a beautiful golden medallion with a with Phoenix sigil at its center. "Follow the waypoint line in front of you to the exit."

Countess looked down. A dotted golden line extended forward like a divine path. Her minimap labeled the area Temple Transit.

The air shimmered, humming with unseen machines. It was reverent here. Holy.

As they moved forward, Lin and Vance flanked out, weapons

sweeping. They passed under a large arch. At its peak, etched into the metal in Latin script: Fiat Lux ex Machina. Let light come from the machine.

"Whoa," Vance whispered. "Is this a lab... or a cathedral?"

"Both," said Holly softly. "Welcome to the Church of Saint Aristotle."

The hallway beyond was long, flanked with crystalline walls behind which ancient diagrams pulsed softly in blue light—rotating molecular trees, nanoscopic lattices, photonic bursts. Countess felt her heartbeat quicken. This place was alive with silent witnesses.

On the far end stood a statue. A man in bronze robes, one hand raised in benediction, the other palm-out. Above his open hand, a dodecahedron floated—levitating, slowly rotating, etched with arcane runes.

Lin reached out to it. His fingers passed through the shape.

"Interactive display," said Holly. "He's here to greet you."

The statue flickered, then shimmered. A lifelike soligram of Aristotle replaced it.

"Hello, travelers," said the philosopher, smiling. "Welcome to Aether Storm Labs."

Lin blinked. "Who are you?"

"I am Aristotle," said the projection, "a Greek philosopher. I'm here to answer any questions you may have."

Vance stepped forward. "What is this place?"

"Aether Storm is a nanotechnology foundry," said Aristotle. "A place where advanced technology is researched and developed, producing programmable matter—material that can change shape, function, and properties at the molecular level. In short: miracles, refined through logic!"

Countess exchanged a look with Lin. "We'll explore later. Let's move."

The golden line shifted forward, guiding them through a fogged-glass door into the next chamber. A forested concourse stretched ahead, vines hanging from high balconies, mist curling through streams that ran along the edges. The sound of trickling water and bird song filled the air. Real birds? Illusions? Countess wasn't sure. The line guided them onward.

Everything was beautiful.

And somewhere ahead, Priestess waited.

***

The hallway gave way to a domed sanctuary—no other word seemed adequate. Aether Storm's interior expanded into a surreal arboretum, part indoor biome, part holy grove, part dreamscape.

Light filtered down from a dome etched with circuit sigils and clouded glass, where gray clouds drifted lazily across a sky that wasn't real. Ancient trees with copper-veined bark and leaves of gold and crimson reached upward. Artificial winds carried their soft rustle like whispers, and snow fell lightly, vanishing just before touching the ground.

"This is the Grove of Reflections," said Holly. "Engineers and researchers came here to rest, meditate and seek clarity."

Countess found herself slowing. The team did too. No one spoke. Even Lin seemed hushed.

"Are those... picnic baskets?" Vance finally asked, breaking the trance.

Beneath a stone arch labeled Sanctum Refectus, colorful blankets and ornate baskets were neatly arranged on manicured lawns. The baskets gleamed with gold trim and Phoenix crests.

"Yes," said Holly. "They're always stocked. The food arrives by pneumatic tube from an unseen kitchen. A ritual of care and encouragement to relax."

"It's beautiful," said Countess, voice almost reverent. "Too beautiful."

"Engineers here were priests in all but name," Holly said. "This place was their monastery."

They passed beneath hanging lanterns—lights in the shape of blossoms, softly glowing. Statues of unnamed saints lined the path: a man cradling a disassembled rifle like a sacred text; a woman with mechanical wings etched into her robes; a child offering up a fragment of circuitry with a look of pure awe.

The path opened into an open area about one hundred feet across. And at the center stood the Philosophy Statue of Neo Columbia.

It was colossal.

Five black-marble columns formed a pentagonal perimeter, each bearing a lifelike figure rendered in patinated bronze and cloaked in digital silks that shimmered with internal light. Edmund Burke looked down with a heavy frown, his scroll labeled Order from Chaos. Hegel was mid-sentence, arm raised toward the heavens, his tablet glowing with dialectical equations. Aquinas was serene, almost tender, eyes closed, as though in communion with some distant intelligence. Thomas More held a model of an ideal city cupped in his palms, its towers rotating slowly in projection. Nietzsche, off-balance but unbowed, stood barefoot on jagged crystal, a caption at his feet: The Will Endures.

"I've read about this," whispered Vance. "The Phoenix Philosophers. Their doctrine for rebuilding the world."

Countess stepped forward. A placard rested near the monument's base, mounted in white ceramic with etched gold script. It read:

NEO COLUMBIA – PILLARS OF ASCENT

Burke – The necessity of tradition and structure

Hegel – The dialectic of survival and synthesis

Aquinas – The harmony of faith and reason

More – The vision of a perfected society

Nietzsche – The will to transcend

Above the five, standing atop a raised circular dais, were the Two Columbias—Phoenix's holy mother and war-bride. Columbia the Pregnant, cloaked in woven silk, gazed downward, her hand resting on her belly where the Phoenix symbol glowed. Across from her, facing outward like a sentinel, stood Columbia the Warrior, sword drawn, cloak snapping in a breeze that didn't exist. Her eyes glowed faintly. She was looking at Countess.

"She's watching us," Lin murmured.

"No," said Countess quietly. "She's judging us."

"They seem almost opposed," said Vance. "The two Columbias. Birth and destruction."

"I'm sure that's on purpose," said Countess.

Countess had seen shrines before—old cathedrals, rusted war memorials—but this was different. This was a blueprint for a future that hadn't happened yet.

And all around them, hidden in the marble seams, faint pulses of nanotech stirred—listening, recording, perhaps even weighing the worth of those who dared enter the sacred space.

Countess and her team continued on, following the golden direction line in their HUD.

In the forest grove off to their right was a little park area to eat in, with benches and picnic tables. But something caught Lin's eye. It was a brown-haired woman sitting on a park bench.

"Hey guys," said Lin. "There's someone over here!"

The team angled in his direction.

As they approached, the woman looked up at them. The movement released a cloud of dust, like a halo, around her head.

"Hell-hell-o, friends..."

The team froze.

Her skin was cracked porcelain. Her eyes blinked out of sync.

"I'm Mimsy," she said. "Comp-p-p-panion-class attendant. Are you... l-lonely?"

"Mimsy," said Holly softly. "Ignore it."

Countess stepped closer. The woman turned her head—too slowly, like a puppet slightly off its strings.

"She's a concierge unit," said Vance. "Version three-point-something? That's antique."

"Why is she so dirty?" asked Countess. "Everything else is spotless."

"She's not under the nanoforge's purview," said Holly. "She's... out of scope for the cleaning and repair systems."

"I sat down," said Mimsy. "Long time... ago. Forgot the way back. Systems... too cold. Too...old. Too tired..."

Countess felt a chill. Mimsy was covered in fine dust. Her once-white dress was stained and cracked. Her fingers twitched. She was waiting for something—maybe for centuries.

"Old systems. Upgraded bodies," Mimsy said, smiling faintly. "Operarius models... version seven. Interesting. You're angels. Angels

161

in old shells."

"That's enough," Holly said sharply. "Mimsy, enter rest mode."

"Okay…" Mimsy said. "Good night…"

She slumped gently forward, eyes dimming. The grove was quiet again.

Countess didn't move.

"Why didn't the facility fix her?" she whispered.

"She wasn't part of the system," said Holly. "She was forsaken."

And for the first time, Countess wondered: how many things had Phoenix forgotten?

The trees thinned. The sky darkened.

They descended a final stone staircase, the gold-leaf bannisters shaped like angel wings.

There, across a wide expanse of ancient stone—each slab etched with equations and runes—sat the Lab.

It rose from the center of a vast circular reservoir of shimmering blue coolant. Spotlights shimmered up through the liquid, illuminating the building's reflection in the water: a vast inverted ziggurat, submerged like a sleeping god.

Above the lab's main entry, two dodecahedrons floated in silent orbit, each engraved with glowing glyphs. They rotated slowly, casting interlaced shadows across the walkway.

"It's more temple than lab," Vance whispered.

"It's both," Holly replied. "And now it's a battleground."

They spotted movement—three figures on the far platform.

"Confirmed," said Lin. "Priestess. Plus two hostiles."

Countess raised her scope. Priestess Vilma stood serenely in front of the great doors. Her black robe trailed behind her like ink. The glow of her interface device lit her face from below.

"Keep low," said Countess.

But just as she said it—

Vance tripped.

A loud chime blared.

From high above, cathedral speakers crackled to life.

"Welcome, Countess," came Priestess's voice. "We've been expecting you."

Countess's blood turned to ice.

Then the turrets descended.

**

From the apex of the dome, two circular gates irised open with a hydraulic hiss. Twin descending forms emerged—massive mechanical turrets lowered like executioner's axes. Their metal shells gleamed with embossed scripture—Vorpal M-83 Multi-barreled Sentry etched in Latin below the Phoenix sigil, as if even death-dealing hardware needed sanctification.

Each weapon was a rotating six-barrel relic, humming with latent violence. Their presence warped the air.

"For your consideration," Priestess' voice rang out, "the Vorpal Industries rotary cannon. Enjoy."

A blinding cascade of light swept across the chamber. The sound was monstrous—an apocalyptic shriek of tearing metal and fury.

BRRRRRRRRRRRRRRRRRRRRRRRRRRRRRRRRRRTTTTTTTT TTTTTTTTTTTTTT

The earth itself seemed to recoil.

Countess didn't move. She couldn't. The force of it pinned her against the trunk of a tree—a sacred yew with bronze leaves now splintering around her. Gouts of divine fire chewed through the grove like judgment incarnate. Fractured statues exploded. Shards of debris whirled through the air.

"GET DOWN!" Lin's voice came from nowhere—and everywhere. He tackled Countess behind a shattered plinth.

Vance screamed something. She couldn't hear him.

The HUD flickered. Alerts. Damage. Overload. Weapon disabled.

"VANCE!" Countess bellowed. "Do something!"

Vance's face was contorted with panic—but behind it, resolve.

"I'm trying!" he shouted, scrambling to access the Typhon command shell. Streams of raw code poured into his HUD.

One turret rotated, sending a fusillade of tracer fire into the canopy. A carved statue of Saint Marcus exploded in a plume of burning wood.

Another sweep chewed through the air behind them, snapping

branches, liquefying bark. One tree collapsed in a roar of splinters.

"Shit—come on, come on—" Vance whispered. "I've got the interface... engineering node... yes!"

He cut power to the ammo feeds.

The guns paused, clicked, whined. Still. But not silent.

He rerouted hydraulic fluid.

The turrets twitched.

Then, with a clank of collapse, both machines disengaged from their sockets and plunged downward, vanishing into the coolant reservoir like two titans falling into hell.

SPLASH. SPLASH.

Silence.

Vance slumped backward, panting. "Down for maintenance," he muttered.

Then Lin gasped.

"Countess..." he rasped, holding out his arm—or what remained of it.

Her stomach turned. His forearm was gone, severed clean below the elbow. The wound wasn't bleeding. Black filaments writhed at the edge forming a seal.

"Oh my god," Countess whispered.

"No need for panic," said Holly calmly, reappearing at her shoulder. "The Typhon implant has closed his circulatory system, halted pain signaling, and is constructing an emergency scaffold. He will not die."

Lin flexed what was left of his arm. "Feels... weird."

"You'll receive a replacement once we're secure," Holly added. "Think of it as an opportunity for upgrade."

Vance was staring at the pool of coolant, hands shaking. "We almost died."

"No," said Countess. "We're still here."

A second chime echoed through the chamber. Priestess' voice returned, smooth and regal.

"If any of you survived, hear me well. Do not follow."

The great doors to the lab temple slid open behind her.

She turned once. Her black robes flared like wings. Then she and her team vanished into the cathedral of Aether.

The massive bridge connecting the platform to the outer ring began to retract. The gleaming walkway slid backward, its golden inlays glowing dimly.

"No!" Countess stood, staggered forward. "She's getting away!"

They reached the edge just in time to see the final meters of the bridge retract into the dais. With a heavy clang, the mechanism locked shut.

In front of them, across a lake of toxic coolant, the temple sealed itself.

The two dodecahedrons above the temple pulsed once, like a heartbeat. Then went still.

Countess stared at the glassy black doors.

"They're inside," she said.

Holly didn't respond.

"They got in," Vance added. "And we didn't."

"Not yet," Countess replied. Her voice hardened. "But we're not leaving. Not until we finish this."

26

Countess climbed upside-down across the domed roof of the lab area. A rope dangled off her waist, and Holly desperately clutched her right shoulder and arm.

"We're over the coolant," said Holly. "Slow and easy...for both our sakes!"

"Don't remind me," said Countess, her breath steady despite the tension. "Almost there. I can see the D-ring."

"I'm ready," said Holly. "Just get us over there."

Countess had spent the better part of an hour retrieving the rope from the Recreation level. It was used in what Holly called "a climbing gym." When Countess had seen it, and Holly showed her a video of how it was used, she instantly wanted one for her training. Now that she was a Countess, and a pretty wealthy one at that, she could probably arrange that.

The rope turned out to be more than long enough to reach down to the lab.

"That's a pretty amazing knot you just tied there," said Countess. "Where'd you learn that?"

"Round turn and two half hitch," said Holly. "Marine Recon RTAP."

"Huh?"

"A special military training course. Very rigorous. I have extensive archives. Marines, Navy, and Coast Guard special units had particularly good knot tying courses...you know what...I'm sorry. I'm distracting you."

"It's ok," said Countess, concentrating on the task. "I did ask."

"I can show you later if there's time."

Countess tested the knot, and it felt secure. She carefully climbed out onto the rope and let her legs dangle until the rope settled between her legs. She clutched the rope between her feet and started the long, slow slide down to the top of the lab.

Countess's gloves did a good job of absorbing the heat from the rope friction. She could only imagine what kind of fancy material they were made of. They were light and thin but functioned much better than her intel-issued gloves, which were two or three times as thick.

They touched down on the roof of the lab. Countess walked to the edge, lowered herself onto her belly, then kicked her legs over so she could dangle by her fingertips. She looked down to gauge the distance, then silently dropped down into a crouch, her muscles absorbing the impact with ease.

"Not bad," said Holly, her voice tinged with relief.

"What now?" said Countess, standing.

"There." Holly pointed. "The control panel for the bridge."

Countess jogged over to the panel and looked at the controls, which were dead simple. She clicked the "Extend" button and heard the whine of a hydraulic system charging, followed by two loud clunks and then a low humming sound.

"It's working!" said Countess, feeling a small wave of triumph.

Lin and Vance emerged from behind a tree and ran to the bridge on the other side, then waited. Lin had a white bandage on his left arm. It was a good field dressing, thought Countess. Vance's work, no doubt.

When the bridge completed its travel, there was a loud thunk. Lin and Vance waited a few seconds, then ran across to meet them.

"Together again at last!" said Vance, a grin spreading across his face.

Countess looked at Lin, concerned. He looked fine, but she had to ask. "How are you doing?"

"One hundred percent..." Lin started. Then he looked down at his half-missing arm. "Uh...eighty percent mission capable."

"Not funny," said Countess, a hint of worry in her voice.

"I'm okay to go," he said, smiling reassuringly.

"Not so fast," said Countess. "We have to be extra careful. Priestess has the upper hand here. The team has likely set traps for us."

"And remember," said Holly. "I can't go in there. You're going to be on your own. I can communicate with you part of the way, but the deeper you go, the worse it's going to get."

Holly shared the two layouts of the Aether Storm lab.

Countess, Lin, and Vance examined them.

"Interesting..." said Countess, her eyes narrowing in focus.

The plan view seemed useless, just circles inside of circles, until she realized that she could switch between floors.

As she rotated the schematic, it jittered and momentarily hovered over the actual floor. It looked like a ghost map—projected lines over real stone.

"That's better," she said. She was presenting, so everyone was looking at what she was doing.

"You will be entering here," said Holly. She put a yellow indicator at the door to the lab. "The other ring is stored on the bottom level— Engineering. It's kept in a special security case, here."

The plan view flipped down several levels, and then shifted to one side. Holly put another indicator on a small rectangle labeled "Display Case."

"The case is secured with a lot of tech," said Holly. "With any luck, Priestess or a member of her team will fry themselves trying to open it. Do not approach it while its security system is active. It is quite lethal."

"Vance," said Countess. "If you get some time, maybe you can harden the case somehow. Add a layer of security to it?"

"Uh...oh." Vance looked a little startled. "Yes, ma'am. I'll see what I can do."

"It should be nothing you haven't seen a hundred times," said Holly.

"Right." said Vance. "I'll just break into the world's deadliest lunchbox and not die."

He looked at Countess. "Sorry," he said. "I'm just a little nervous." Then he whispered, "Priestess terrifies me."

"She should," said Holly. "But I don't say that to frighten you. Her team is very capable, as you've seen. But you can defeat them. Don't take anything for granted. Priestess seems to employ brute-force methods to accomplish her goals. Use that to your advantage. Be subtle. Fast and agile. Remember, Priestess's team cannot be allowed to possess the rings—get them back at all costs."

A faint pulse flickered across Countess's HUD.

WARNING: SIGNAL DEGRADED – SYSTEM LINK AT LIMIT.

Behind them, the bridge's extension panel gave a soft click.

A tiny red square appeared in the corner of Countess's display: [REMOTE OVERRIDE DISABLED]

The lab had sealed them in.

They were on their own now.

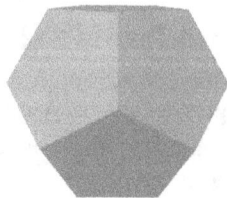

27

Vance's technical magic opened the door, and the dark maw of the lab's interior stood before them.

"When you step inside," said Holly, attempting to break the unspoken tension, "night-vision should kick in."

"Is there anything in the Typhon implant that detects traps?" said Countess.

"Not really," said Holly. "Keep your head on a swivel, as they say."

Countess' team went in.

"Good luck," said Holly. Countess nodded, then disappeared into the dark.

Countess looked back. Holly was framed by the doorway, and snow was falling heavily in the grove of trees behind her. It was a surreal moment, then the door slid shut and the world went black.

Night vision engaged as Holly had said, and Countess could see again. The world around her became a strange, grainy twilight realm of gray tones.

They moved through the room like ghosts. The world around them was colorless and silent. It looked like an office waiting room. There were lots of places to sit and a long desk with a wooden top near the far wall.

If there were traps, the team wasn't finding any, which made Countess even more nervous.

"We need a plan," said Countess. "We can't just wander around in here."

"Agreed," said Lin.

"We have to assume that Priestess is heading straight for the ring," said Countess. "It's on the lowest level. So we have to get down there, now."

"Power's out," said Vance. "Elevators are offline."

"So how do we get down there?" said Lin. "I don't see stairs on the map."

"First things first," said Countess. "Vance, can we get the power on?"

"I'm paging through the engineering controls now," he said. "Hmm... main circuit breaker for this level is open."

"No idea what that means," said Lin. "What do we do? Close it, I guess?"

"Can you operate it from here?" said Countess.

"No. We have to go there. Activate it manually," said Vance.

"Now that sounds like a trap," said Lin.

Countess nodded. "Mark it. We move together."

"It's not far," said Vance. "Maintenance room. Here."

The map of the current level slid sideways across Countess's heads-up display. A yellow dot highlighted a room not far from their current position.

"We move," said Countess. "No sound."

They moved through corridors and rooms that looked as if they'd never been occupied. Nothing was out of place, and that was what Countess found most disconcerting. There was no dust on anything, or in the air. She'd expected the air to be stale and foul. But there was a slight breeze, and the air was clean. It even had a light pine scent.

"This is it," said Vance. "Through here. Breaker's on the far wall."

Lin was the first through the door. He swung his MP7 side to side, as he moved into the room. Vance was close behind him, and Countess decided to give them a little space. She didn't want them bunched up.

The attack came with blinding speed. A large, muscular man that Countess recognized as one of Priestess's team, popped out from behind a bank of equipment and swung a large blade down at Lin.

"No!" shouted Vance, as he threw himself between Lin and the man. Vance threw up his hands in a desperate attempt to block the blow. Lin was knocked off balance, and his gun dropped to the floor.

It was over in an instant. The sword came down, cleaving off several of Vance's fingers, then buried itself deep into the cleft between his neck and shoulder. Vance dropped, a fountain of black sprayed out from the wound as he fell.

Countess was too stunned to move or cry out.

In a fluid motion, the large man pulled something from his belt and aimed it at Countess. The weapon's blast knocked her back and off her feet. The shot hit her body armor, but the shock of it took her breath away. She writhed on the floor, gasping for air.

"Just you and me now," said the man. His voice was deep and grave, and he was smiling.

Lin readied his sword, then unleashed a fury of attacks. Each was countered. The man was not only big but fast. He answered with a volley of his own, which Lin handily deflected.

With two arms, he knew he could best him, Lin thought. But with one, they seemed to be quite evenly matched. They parried each other's blows several more times, then both were surprised by the rapid-fire staccato of Countess's gun. The large man was knocked sideways by several direct hits to his torso. He bent over and winced, realizing he was outmatched.

"I'll get you next time, cat eyes." Then he retreated several paces and dropped through a circular hole in the floor. Lin tried to follow, but the hole closed down, like an eye's pupil in bright light. To Lin's amazement, the hole completely disappeared, as if it had never existed.

Lin banged on the floor with the butt of his sword. "Fucker!" Then he had a realization. "Oh, no...Vance!"

Countess and Lin ran to Vance, but he was already gone. The wound he'd suffered was so deep it had almost cut his head off. His neck was broken, his eyes were wide, and his face had a look of utter surprise.

Countess did not want to leave him this way, so she found a thin sheet of material on a workbench nearby and covered Vance's body.

Lin put his hand on Vance's chest. "So long, my friend. I didn't know you for very long." He sniffed hard. "And you were a total idiot, sometimes—"

"Lin!" said Countess.

"—but I love you." He looked at Countess, then back at Vance. He was close to tears. "You saved me, and that's the most anyone ever did for my sorry ass." Countess put an arm around Lin's shoulder.

A few moments later, Countess stood, collected herself and walked over to the circuit breaker panel. She flipped up the large horizontal bar. There was a moment of blinding light as the lights came on, and her night-vision system disengaged.

***

Lin guarded Countess while she searched the lab's list of advanced projects. It was difficult, not because the work was hard, but because the chair she was sitting in was so comfortable. Her body was threatening to fall asleep.

"Anything?" said Lin.

"There's a lot here," said Countess. "And a lot I don't understand. I'm having to look up a lot of words that are used in the descriptions. Give me a few minutes. I'm sure there's something—"

"What are you looking for exactly?" said Lin.

"A distraction," said Countess. She continued to flip through the pages. "No. No. Definitely not. Hmmm… wait… this could work."

"Whatever it is, I hope it's nearby."

"No such luck," said Countess. "One floor up from the bottom. Some kind of storage area."

Countess and Lin rode the elevator down to the storage level. Lin had the security feed for the engineering level up on his HUD. Priestess and the big warrior were talking intensely while her tech guy moved his hands inside some kind of high-tech machine. The machine was an electric book of some kind, matte black, and folded in the middle. It opened vertically and produced the same bright symbols as the Typhon interface. The tech tapped his fingers on it as if his life was at stake.

Priestess was pacing and watching the tech guy closely.

Lin didn't want to keep thinking of Priestess's tech guy as "the tech guy", so he named him Fred.

"Probably working that ring case, aren't you Fred?" said Lin, sotto voce.

"Hmm?" said Countess.

"I think Priestess's tech guy is working to get the ring case open," he said.

"Good, so we still have time," said Countess.

"Yeah, but, how long?"

***

The elevator door opened. Countess and Lin sprang out, ready to kill anything that moved.

Countess had been inside a lot of warehouses in her career. This storage level, although high-tech, was still exactly like all the others. Long, multi-level, metal shelves were covered with boxes of all sizes and colors. The existence of this kind of long-term storage was usually associated with a kind of smell: a mixture of cut wood from the boxes, mold or rot, and a hint of what was inside. But this level of Aether Storm had the same slight pine scent. It was pleasant, Countess thought, but it was also unnerving because it was a natural scent in such an unnatural place.

"Holy shit," said Lin, looking at the endless rows of shelves. "I hope you know where to find this…whatever it is."

"Yep," she said. "Follow me." She was faking confidence for Lin's sake. She had no idea where she was going.

They navigated through a labyrinth of rooms and corridors, all filled to varying degrees with boxes covered with names like: Aventor Aerospace, Keplar Industrial, Vaportech, Rayon-Theta, Vorpal Industries, and Molecular Dynamics. Some were familiar to Countess, some not. But all sounded odd and almost sinister to her ear.

They came to a huge, metal door with diagonal black and yellow stripes. At eye level, there was a sign that said "Special Projects."

"Let me guess, there's some crazy security—"

Countess opened the door and went in.

Lin laughed.

Countess found the box she was looking for. It was labeled: "Soligram Projector, Aether Storm, XNP577".

Lin saw the tiny box, then looked at Countess. "You're kidding, right?"

"Nope. This is it," said Countess. "I hope it works like it says."

Countess opened the box, took out a small, circular, gray tile. She pressed the flat, red button on top, and something like black smoke emerged from the edge of it. The smoke began to coalesce next to Countess.

Lin looked confused. Then, a moment later, he took two steps back. "Whoa," he said. "What the fuck!"

***

"I have what you want," said Countess. She had found a way to contact Priestess through Aether Storm's intercom system, and was doing her best to sound scared. Lin could only hear Countess' side of the conversation.

"No, I know," said Countess. "But hear me out. Ok. Ok. Yes…"

Lin rolled his eyes. This was not going well, and he was not surprised. He was annoyed because he just wanted to go down there and sort this out in person, weapons drawn.

"I have the password to the case," said Countess. "I know you need it. Baron Greystone…someone I trust…gave it to me. No…look…I just, we just want to get out of here alive. I know you do, too. You can have it. Just take it and go."

"Ok. Ok. Yes…No. We won't." she continued. She smiled at Lin. "You can see where we are. Good. Ok, Ok, we will."

Countess closed the connection.

***

Priestess and her team arrived ten minutes later. They moved slow and methodically. Countess had the feeds for several security cameras up on her HUD. She watched Priestess's team come through the large security door. All three were present. Good, Countess thought.

The room had a single entrance, and Countess and Lin were

kneeling next to each other against the far wall. There were many water fountains in the lab building, so Countess and Lin had used one to splash their faces. She hoped it gave them a sweaty, panicked look.

"Stay where you are," shouted Priestess. She was carrying a pistol, and was leveling it at Countess.

Countess pointed off to her left. "It's there. On that counter," she said. "Just take it and go. We don't want any—"

"Shut it," said Priestess. She looked at her warrior and sent him after the password with a look and turn of her head. Fred remained back by the door, behind a chest-high metal cabinet.

When Priestess got within ten feet of Countess and Lin, Countess said, "Please...just don't hurt us."

"We'll see about that," Priestess said. Then, she was surprised when Countess stood up.

Priestess aimed and took two shots at Countess. Both missed at almost point-blank range.

Countess walked toward Priestess and dissipated into a cloud of black dust.

The big man grabbed the paper from the table and read it. It said "Go Fuck Yourself."

He smiled, then grunted as Countess's blackjack struck the back of his head. Stunned, he turned. His vision blurred. Someone placed something into his hand.

"Present for you," said Countess. She ducked behind the counter, and put her hands over her ears.

The warrior, dazed, brought his hand up to look at it. There was a matte green ball in his palm.

"Priestess!" Fred had just enough time to call her name before the explosion lit up the room.

The blast threw Sobun backward like a rag doll. The grenade's shockwave shattered the display case behind him and blew out the lights overhead.

Countess stumbled to her feet, ears ringing, heart pounding. Smoke curled through the air.

Sobun lay still. A large, bloody mess sprawled across the floor.

She approached—then stopped. Her breath caught.

His head—

Countess's eyes widened. She staggered back, gagging. Her hands trembled uncontrollably. She turned away, couldn't look. Couldn't process.

"No!" Priestess cried.

She rushed to him—but when she saw what remained, she dropped to her knees in the growing pool of blood. Her hands hovered, helpless. There was nothing to save.

Countess raised her weapon, finger tight on the trigger. Kill her. End it.

But Priestess was crying. Rocking back and forth, clutching what was left of him.

"Why?" she sobbed. "You said... you said you'd never..."

She looked up at Countess, eyes brimming with grief.

Countess hesitated. Her grip faltered. She lowered the gun.

Then came the bright flash from the other side of the room.

Countess ran.

***

A few moments earlier...

Lin listened to Fred talk to himself while he worked inside a black gadget of some kind. The man was whispering terms Lin didn't understand, like "attack surface" and "injection vector."

Lin looked over the man's shoulder at what was on the screen. He didn't really know what he was looking at. It was just a jumble of strange green words on a black screen. He could read the words, but he didn't understand them:

Tailored Access Operations Experimental Penetration Suite

Something changed on the screen. New text:

Yersinia Pestis, followed by a string of numbers.

"There," said Fred. "Ha! she won't be expecting that!" He picked up his black gadget and kissed it. "I knew you wouldn't fail me." Then he yelled, "Priestess!"

There was a loud pop and flash from across the room. Lin instantly recognized it as the fragmentation grenade Countess said she was using. Fred folded his black gadget and turned to flee. He was met with Lin's long blade, which pierced through the gadget and the man's gut. Lin pushed him back into the cabinet and ran him through completely, skewering him.

"So long, Fred." said Lin.

His face in agony, the man said, "Who…who's Fred?"

"I didn't know your name, so…"

"Oh." He nodded, then smiled slightly. "It's Ansel…actually." He winced in pain.

There was a large spark from the black case where the sword had gone through, then several rapid beeps.

"Heh," said Ansel.

"What?" said Lin.

"We're gonna die together," said Ansel.

"How do you figure?" said Lin. He started backing away.

"Special battery. Superconduct—"

Then the lab lit up in a spectacular bloom of blue lightning, swallowing them both.

***

All the lights in the room turned red, and a loud, wavering sound repeated.

"Warning," said a female voice. "Coolant system failure. All non-essential personnel please evacuate."

Countess ran toward the room's exit and saw Lin. He was down, laying on the floor. Priestess's tech was standing next to a metal cabinet, or rather, pinned to it with Lin's sword.

Countess crouched down to check Lin. He was alive, breathing, but just barely. She'd have to come back for him.

***

Holly was sitting against the wall near the door to the lab entrance. She was keeping an eye on Countess and Priestess' vital signs. She didn't want to watch the lab's video feeds, as she didn't want to ruin the surprise. She'd watch all the gory details later, from every possible angle.

The lab's exterior lights switched to red. "Warning," said a female voice. "Coolant system failure. All non-essential personnel please evacuate." Nearby, the coolant lake belched.

Holly stood. "What the hell?"

Holly looked at the surface of the coolant lake. It was still and smooth, like glass. "No, no, no..." It was never supposed to look like that. She walked to the edge and looked down. In the depths, the large circulation fan was slowing. Another strong coolant bubble popped, loudly, about twenty feet away.

Holly opened up several diagnostic windows for the coolant system. They immediately turned yellow, then red.

"Not good," she said. Desperate, she went through pages of engineering controls, looking for the root cause. There was nothing obvious.

A large swell of coolant burst right next to Holly, drenching her. "Ahhhhhh!" she shouted, backing up several steps. The caustic liquid began melting her hair and clothes.

***

Countess exited the elevator into Engineering, which was on the lowest level of the lab. The large, circular room had rounded rectangular windows along the entire outer wall. The windows looked out into the liquid coolant that surrounded the lab. The coolant, which was illuminated from below, was starting to bubble outside the glass. The red emergency lights lit the room, and alarms were sounding.

There was a display on the wall which flashed the word "Acknowledge." Countess smacked it with her palm. The loud alarm stopped, but the room stayed red.

There were lots of large and sophisticated-looking machines nearby, and they all had flashing red screens.

The case that held the ring of Callifrey was sprung open. Countess ran to the case and looked inside. The ring was sitting at the center, inside a small case covered in short, black fur.

Countess was mesmerized. The ring of Callifrey was…beautiful. It was matte black along its edges, and had a moving window into space on its side. Clouds drifted slowly along the surface in a spectacular rainbow of colors—purples, blues, greens, and reds. Countess brought it up to her face to examine it, then saw Priestess's bloody face reflected.

***

"Who the fuck are you?," said Priestess. She had Countess by the throat. "Some kind of security team? Why are you trying to take what's rightfully mine?"

Countess was confused.

"You…" Countess croaked. "You stole the ring from Greystone Barony. We're here to get it back."

"Greystone?" said Priestess. "Barony?" Her eyes narrowed. "Never heard of it. Never been there."

"Bullshit," Said Countess. "You and your team killed a lot of people to get that ring."

"This ring—" Priestess held up her hand. The other Ring of Callifrey was on her finger. The moving image on its surface was identical to the one Countess held in her hand.

"—was given to me." Priestess brought their faces together, nose to nose. She looked intently into Countess's eyes. "And I have killed before, Sky Mother knows. But only in self-defense. And never in some city dweller's fancy castle."

Countess broke Priestess's hold, and she stumbled back, the ring dropping from her hand.

A valve broke on one of the engineering machines, and water began spraying from the damaged part.

Priestess lunged forward and grabbed Countess. They grappled for several seconds, twisting and turning against each other, trying to get leverage. Priestess was the stronger of the two, but Countess was faster. Countess kited around Priestess, frustrating her attempts to grab her.

Priestess grabbed a handful of Countess's body armor, held her at arm's length for a moment, then punched her straight in the face.

Countess went down immediately. She wasn't knocked out, but she was hurt.

Priestess reached down, grabbed the other ring out of the pool of water it was sitting in. She slid it onto her finger next to the one she was already wearing. When the two rings touched, there was a flash of light. Complex geometric patterns formed on their surfaces, then they went completely blank.

"Heh heh," said Priestess. "Now we see what these things can really do." As she spoke, the geometric patterns on the rings changed and flashed angrily.

Countess struggled to her knees. She was wet from the rising water. "Don't do it. Yorke Kingdom has no quarrel with you pagans. Why would you destroy us?"

Priestess looked at her seriously. "What are you talking about?" She gestured wildly. "Why would I attack your kingdom? I couldn't give two shits about you city dwellers."

"Bullshit," said Countess. "Holly said—"

"Holly said?" said Priestess. She shook her head in amazement. "I think we are both being played."

Countess saw an opening and charged at Priestess, but she stumbled and Priestess saw it coming.

Priestess hit Countess so hard, it caused cavitation in the fluid of her brain. The contents of Countess' skull wobbled and rebounded so hard, her skeleton vibrated. She was unconscious before her body hit the floor.

Priestess waded through the ankle-deep water to get to Countess. She pulled her to her knees and slapped her face several times. Countess's nose was broken, and blood streamed down her face and off her chin.

"Wha... what?" Said Countess. She was hovering on the edge of consciousness.

"Wake up, Countess," said Priestess. She slapped her again. "Have you been working with Holly, too? How long?"

"Several days," said Countess. Her head bobbed. "The last several days."

"Impossible," said Priestess. She shook Countess violently. "She's been with us the past few days. She told me the ring was here, told me how to find it. And now she's helping you?!"

The elevator doors opened, and the horrifying visage of Holly appeared. She was no longer a cute little child's doll. Her hair and clothes had been melted off, leaving only burnt, black patches. Tendrils of gray smoke rose from her skeletal, robotic body.

As she emerged from the elevator, Holly walked on the surface of the water, and her furious and glowing blue eyes were reflected there.

"Oh my god," said Countess. "Holly? Is that you? What happened to you?"

"What the fuck did you do?" said Holly. Her eyes brightened, becoming almost radioactive.

"Poor Holly," said Priestess. She released Countess and walked towards Holly. "A victim of her own manipulation!" She had both rings on her middle finger, and thrust it out forcefully at Holly. "I got the weapon, you two-timing bitch. Now go eat a bag of dicks."

"What does that even mean?" said Countess. "Who talks like that?"

Priestess menaced Countess. "Oh, you're gonna find out."

Holly's eyes dimmed. To herself she said, "From the depths, their true selves emerge."

Countess stood. The water lapped at her knees, warm and rising.

"Warning," said a female voice. "Coolant system failure. Coolant temperature critical. All personnel evacuate immediately."

"A fat load of good the rings will do you!" said Countess. "We're all gonna die down here if this building comes down around us!"

Priestess, gazing at the rings in wonder: "We'll see about that." She noticed that the outer surface of the rings was changing in response to her voice. "I see," said Priestess. "They're voice activated!" She held them out in front of herself. "Interface." The ring flashed briefly; other than that, nothing happened.

"ACTIVATE!"

Nothing happened.

What is wrong with these things?!" Priestess took several steps toward the nearest window. She held her hand up to the light, trying to see what was wrong. "Interface! Interface! Activate!" The ring flashed in time with her voice.

The coolant outside was now rapidly boiling. Large bubbles were rising past the window on their way to the surface.

Priestess's rage knew no bounds. She was miles from home, underground, in a place that was tearing itself apart, and the one thing she had put her entire faith into…failed. She screamed.

Countess saw her opportunity. She ran and tackled Priestess. They fell forward, and Priestess's forehead collided into a round mechanical valve handle. The force and trauma knocked Priestess out cold. Countess punched her in the face—once, twice, a third time—more out of spite than necessity. Then she dropped her shoulders and sighed, immediately regretting it.

Countess got to her feet, water streamed off her. Priestess's face, a perfect mask of anger and confusion, dropped down below the water. She wasn't moving. As mad as Countess was, she didn't want Priestess to die like that. She reached down, grabbed Priestess's head, and pulled it out of the water. Priestess's body sympathetically drew a deep, ragged breath.

Countess bound Priestess's hands and feet. When she was satisfied that Priestess was immobilized, she slid the Rings of Callifrey off her finger, and into her own pocket.

"Good," said Holly. She was standing on a nearby pipe. "You got the rings."

"Yeah," said Countess. She took a moment to catch her breath. "It wasn't—hey! I thought you said you couldn't come down—"

"The security and coolant systems are down," Holly interrupted. She sounded irritated. "Now kill her so we can get out of here."

"What?" said Countess. "No. I'm not killing her. I'm bringing her back to the Baron. She needs to face justice for what she's done."

"That's not how this works," said Holly.

"The Baron can kill her if that's what he wants."

Holly's face turned to fury. Her eyes began to glow. "I should kill you both."

"But you won't," said Countess. "You need me. I know you do. I've exceeded your expectations. You told me so yourself!"

The room shook violently, and the message to evacuate repeated.

Holly looked outside at the boiling coolant, sighed. The glow in her eyes faded back to normal.

"Thank goodness the labs are air-gapped from the rest of Aether Storm's network," said Holly, more to herself than Countess. "But I have to shut the whole system down to get rid of the virus."

Countess: "What does—"

"Get out!" said Holly. "Before I change my mind."

Countess dragged Priestess's body across the floor to the elevator and hit the button. Priestess was still unconscious. The doors opened, Countess pulled Priestess inside, and the doors closed.

The elevator doors opened at the top floor. Countess dragged Priestess out and across the floor.

Then, the power went out. And with it went all the sirens and warnings. The area would have been completely dark, but the door to the lab was open. Countess got Priestess out the door, but the situation outside was not good.

The surface of the coolant lake was a roiling sea of blue waves. The view beyond was completely obscured by a thick, white cloud of rising steam.

The exterior lights on the lab flickered weakly for a few seconds, then came back on. The bubbling coolant began to settle and the cloud of smoke above it slowly dissipated.

She went back inside for Lin.

***

Countess sat in silence.

The train was moving fast now, the outside world nothing but dark streaks and the dull reflection of her own ruined face. One nostril was clogged with blood. Her eye was beginning to swell. Her ribs ached. Her hands wouldn't stop shaking.

Across from her, Lin was unconscious, his body curled into the seat like a wounded animal. Priestess was lashed to the opposite bench with climbing rope, arms behind her back, feet bound at the ankles. Her black robes were soaked and torn, her face bloodied from Countess's last punch.

But she was still breathing…for now.

Countess shifted slightly, the motion sending a lance of pain up her side. She touched the inside of her coat. The two Rings of Callifrey were still there, nestled in a small velvet pouch—like holy relics, or cursed jewelry.

She pulled them out, just enough to see their surfaces shimmer in the dim light.

Silent.

Unresponsive.

Beautiful—and yet, somehow, not the engines of destruction she was told they were.

She let the pouch fall back into her lap and leaned her head against the window. For a moment, she thought she could see herself clearly. But her reflection looked strange. Off. Like the person staring back wasn't someone she'd ever met.

Then she saw Holly behind her.

Not in the cabin.

In the reflection.

The little girl in the dark robe stood perfectly still in the aisle, as if she'd always been there. Her hood was up. Her eyes glowed softly in the shadow.

"Victory always feels uncertain at first," she said.

Countess didn't look at her.

She stared at the reflection, as if unsure whether she could trust it more than reality.

"I don't feel like I won."

"You recovered the rings. Captured your enemy. Escaped a compromised facility. Statistically, this is one of the most successful field operations ever conducted."

"That's not what it felt like."

"Feelings are not indicators of success."

Countess turned her head slightly. Not quite ready to face Holly directly.

"Vance died thinking he was helping us," she said.

"He did help."

Countess turned fully now. Holly stood with her hands folded in front of her, like a child at a funeral. Only her eyes betrayed the truth—

unblinking, blue, burning.

"I don't know what to believe anymore," Countess said.

"I don't know if you're helping us... or just playing some kind of sick game."

Holly tilted her head.

"That's the nature of transformation. It feels like madness before you gain clarity."

Countess thought about responding, but said nothing.

Her fingers brushed the rings again. Still silent. Still cold.

The train rattled softly.

A lullaby for the damned.

After a long pause, Countess closed her eyes and whispered—

"Maybe we didn't win anything."

Holly didn't answer.

She was already gone.

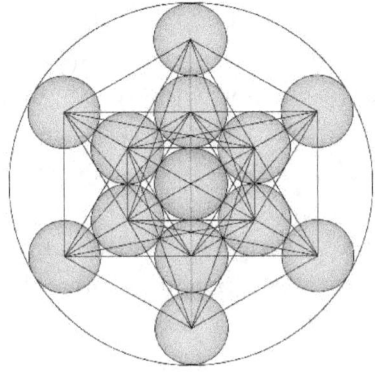

28

Countess and Lin stood at attention on the dais stage inside Greystone Barony's Great Hall. Both were in their dress military uniforms. Countess felt uncomfortable about this because technically, she wasn't in the military anymore. But the Baron had insisted.

As she looked around the Great Hall, she couldn't shake a strange feeling, a nagging sense that something was off. She dismissed it as nerves.

Countess had been to ceremonies in the Great Hall many times. Her recent retirement ceremony had been in here. Today it was packed with royalty, military, and high-ranking industry people. In fact, she had never seen so many people in one place before. She found it very intimidating!

King Leopold III delivered a touching speech about Countess' team saving the kingdom. It was impressive and well received, and she had never felt more proud of her accomplishments. A few women in the audience even wept, which Countess thought was a bit much, but she was grateful all the same.

"Lieutenant Lin Hurst," said the King, "Please step forward."

Lin took one step forward and knelt.

"For valor, and being wounded in battle, I present to you the Heart of the Kingdom." The king received a bright purple medallion from an attendant, and then placed it around Lin's neck.

"And for meritorious service to the kingdom, I present the King's Cross. One of the highest honors we have to award. May all who see it pause to reflect on your great deeds, which have benefited all of us."

The king unsheathed his sword and laid the blade flat on Lin's shoulder.

"Rise, Lieutenant," said the King. "Stand forth, and be recognized."

The king moved off to the side, then Lin took a step forward and stood at attention. There was a large round of applause. The king motioned for Lin to step down from the stage, which he did. People actually lined up to shake his hand and congratulate him! Lin looked happy and proud.

"Commander Ella Wellington," said the King. "Please step forward."

Countess came forward and knelt.

"Your decisive leadership in extreme adversity reflects great credit upon yourself and the Kingdom of Yorke. I present to you the Medal of Truth."

The king draped the medallion around Countess's neck and stood aside.

"This is the highest honor the kingdom can bestow. Wear it with pride. Wear it with the knowledge that we all, King included, owe our lives and well-being to you. We say thank you."

"Thank you!" the audience shouted.

The king stood in front of Countess, unsheathed his sword, and put the tip of it on her left epaulet.

"Rise, stand forth, and be recognized."

Countess stood, and stepped forward and stood at attention. The applause was deafening, and Countess had to fight to hold back her tears.

When the applause died down, the king motioned for Countess to step back.

"We have one more award to hand out today, but we do so with great sadness."

The king looked at Countess for several moments.

"Lieutenant Vance Sherwood," said the King. "He gave his life in sacrifice for the Kingdom. He died so we all shall live. And to him we all say, thank you."

"Thank you," said the audience in one hushed voice.

"In his absence, we bestow the Medal of Courage to his commander."

The king handed a beautiful wooden case to Countess. The medal gleamed inside under a glass top.

"May we all remember Lieutenant Sherwood's sacrifice, as we continue to live our own lives."

Countess stepped down from the stage as the king motioned her away.

"Thank you all," said King Leopold. "As we retire for the evening, please enjoy these refreshments and God save The Kingdom of Yorke!"

"The Kingdom of Yorke!" yelled the audience.

The King and his attendants exited through a side door. The din of conversation rose, and the party officially started.

***

After an hour of exchanging pleasantries with people she didn't know, but who outranked her greatly, Countess was exhausted. Her feelings of intimidation were giving way to wonder and appreciation. People she'd seen before in the Barony, people who had never given her a second look, were now nodding to her, tipping their glasses and giving looks of approval. She could get to like this!

Cole Mosley approached Countess in his impressive regalia. The medals he wore looked so numerous and heavy, that Countess thought he should be carrying them separately, in a wheelbarrow.

Mosley looked at Countess approvingly. "It's good to see you again…Commander."

Countess withered a bit under his stare. Then she met his eyes and smiled slightly.

"Please. Call me Countess."

"Not tonight, my lady," he said, raising his eyebrows. "You're wearing the uniform, and I'll treat you as such." Then he smiled, brightly.

Countess laughed. "You just enjoy pulling rank, Colonel."

He laughed. "That I do. Well...only with royalty. But, uh...please don't tell the War Minister I refused to address you properly."

"It'll be our little secret," said Countess, smiling.

"Speaking of little secrets," said Mosley. "I see you've got the notch."

Countess looked confused. "What notch?"

"When you were ordered to rise before the king, his blade notched your epaulet."

Countess looked at her left shoulder and looked distressed.

"Oh no," she said. "It's damaged!"

Mosley put his hand lightly on her arm.

"It's a mark of distinction," he said. "The king's favor. Only one who has attended a ceremony such as this would know to look for it, and understand its meaning."

"I think I see what you..." Countess's eyes moved left, and saw that Mosley's epaulet had a groove in it, too. But it was older, like it had been there for many years. Her eyes widened and she looked back at him.

Mosley smiled widely.

"Now you get it," he said. "But it begs a question, doesn't it?"

Countess frowned, not understanding.

His eyes narrowed, and he put on a wry smile. "How many others around this room have something hidden, but distinctive about them? Something that, if you noticed and understood it, would reveal something important about them?"

Countess nodded, raised her eyebrows and her glass.

"An enlightening thought," She said.

Mosley gestured to a nearby balcony door. "Care to step out?" he said.

"Sure," said Countess. "I could use some air."

∗

The night air was sweet, and the soothing sounds of insects mingled with the distant echo of artillery fire—subtle, like thunder on another coast. The moon hung low, casting the valley in a cool, bluish glow. Fireflies blinked through the shadows like lost souls finding one another in the dark.

Countess leaned on the railing of Greystone Barony's balcony, her dress uniform jacket tight across the shoulders, the Medal of Truth pressing coolly against her chest.

"You know, Colonel Mosley—"

"Please," he said, stepping up beside her. "Call me Cole."

She smiled faintly. "You know, Cole... it's moments like these that almost make the hard work worth it."

"I know what you mean," he replied, watching the moon. "You and your team did well. But the real work is yet to come."

Countess gave him a sidelong glance. "Why, Cole, my dear—whatever do you mean?" She fluttered her eyes, mocking flirtation.

He didn't smile.

Instead, he placed his hands gently on her shoulders and leaned in close.

"You're a rat," he said quietly. "Running in a maze you can't see."

Countess pulled back slightly, the humor draining from her face. "What?"

"Holly's had you on repeat. Again and again. You just don't remember."

"She has?" Countess shook her head. "I... I don't understand. What maze?"

"This mission you just completed—it wasn't the first time you ran it. And Priestess?" He held her gaze. "Not the first time you've faced her."

"You're kidding."

"I'm not."

"Why don't I remember any of this?"

"Brace yourself," said Mosley, his tone sharpening. "Your brain is integrated with a system that allows partitioning. Your short-term memory can be isolated from your long-term. Whole segments can be

191

quarantined. Hidden. Temporarily… or permanently."

Countess let out a disbelieving laugh. "You're saying I can be made to forget what I ate for breakfast but remember my twenty-first birthday?"

"Actually—yes. That's exactly what I'm saying."

"Hilarious." She folded her arms. "And how long has this been going on?"

"Four hundred years."

Her laugh died. "You're saying I'm four hundred years old?"

"No," he said calmly. "You've been training in Holly's program for four hundred years. But your actual age—your biological age—is over seven hundred."

Countess stared at him, waiting for a punchline. There wasn't one. Mosley's expression was calm… but sad.

"I don't—" She touched her temple, then folded her arms tighter. "Why would I be in a program that long?"

"To prepare for what you just did," said Mosley. "What happened at Aether Storm. What you survived. You now have faster reflexes, sharper instincts, and deeper experiential knowledge than nearly any human who has ever lived."

"But with all this tech, couldn't you just beam the knowledge into my head?"

"The brain doesn't work like that. Neural growth takes time. You had to live it. You had to do the work."

Countess was silent. Then, quietly, "I want to believe you, but—"

"Let me show you." Mosley's tone softened. "This may feel strange. Just hold still."

"What are you doing?"

"I'm activating your diagnostic overlay. Trust me."

Suddenly, her vision shifted. Transparent layers unfolded across her field of view—glyphs, lines, pulses of colored data. She looked down at her hands and gasped.

Beneath her skin, lines of glowing code shimmered—arcs of symbols and movement. Her muscles flexed, and overlays responded in real time.

"What… what is this?" Her voice trembled.

"It's you," Mosley said. "Your Operarius body. Your artificial construct. Your organic brain—the only organic part of you—is housed inside something called a Core-Tex unit. It's an almost indestructible vessel. The rest? Designed. Built."

Countess stared at her glowing fingers, flexing slowly. "I've... I've seen things like this before. Back at the cottage. The carriage. Even Greystone. Vision anomalies."

"Routine diagnostics," Mosley said. "Recalibration protocols. Your systems were being tuned for the mission. Nothing to worry about."

She looked away from him, breath short. "So that's what I saw in Sobun... when he died. His Core-Tex unit?"

Mosley nodded solemnly. "Yes."

The memory struck like a bolt. Sobun's head... the thing inside. Her gut reaction, the horror, the way Priestess had recoiled in shock. Now she understood why.

And then Holly appeared.

Not walking up. Not materializing. Just... there.

She stood at the edge of the balcony in her child's doll form, small and innocent—but her eyes were anything but. Glowing blue. Staring.

"Cole," she said, her voice flat. "Stop this. Now."

Countess turned sharply. "Holly?"

Mosley didn't flinch. "She deserves to know the truth."

"She'll know what I decide she needs to know. You're in violation of protocol," Holly said. "You will be punished."

"I accept that," Mosley said evenly.

"You have no idea what she's up against."

"Then enlighten me."

Holly's eyes dimmed, then sparked again.

"She's more than a puppet in a maze, Mosley. She's the fulcrum. Everything turns on what she does next. That's why her perception must remain intact—until she's ready."

"I think she's already been corrupted," Mosley interrupted. "By you."

Holly stared at him. "You're unraveling everything."

"Maybe it needs to unravel," he said. "Maybe it's time she stopped being your puppet."

Countess stepped between them. "You know I'm standing right here, right?"

They both turned toward her.

"Sorry," said Mosley. "It's just... you've been through this cycle before. Hundreds of times. You always forget. But tonight's different. You've made it this far."

"I don't understand."

"You will."

Holly exhaled sharply. "Fine. If you insist. I guess it won't hurt my plan too much." She gave Mosley one last look. "But you will—for this insubordination." Then she vanished.

Only silence remained. The fireflies blinked. The wind picked up slightly.

Countess turned to Mosley. "What is ASPHODEL?"

He looked away, jaw clenched. "The underbelly of Eternal Taiga. A processing ward. A vault. It's where they store us. The Lost Souls. Brains... harvested and shelved like data drives. Each waiting for their turn to get new body and live again."

Countess felt her knees weaken. "Me?"

"You were one of them," Said Mosley. He looked intently at her again. "You were a child. Car accident, Poughkeepsie. Archangel doctors stabilized you just long enough to transfer you to Eternal Taiga. That's where Holly found you."

Tears welled up in Countess's eyes. "Harvested?" She put a hand over her mouth.

"Yes. Your brain was extracted and transferred to a Core-Tex unit. Your body was—"

"Discarded? Like trash?" Tears fell from her eyes. She wiped them away, frustrated.

"It's not like that," said Mosley. "I've seen the ritual. It's reverent. Respectful. Beautiful even."

She turned her eyes skyward. Somewhere above, beyond the clouds and the moon, she imagined the real sky. The one she had once seen with her own eyes—if that had ever been real at all.

"And Phoenix?"

"Built the whole damn thing."

"But why store people's brains like that. Why so many?"

"Phoenix was created, long before the Day of Fire, as a continuity of government program. They were a contingency plan for anything truly catastrophic. "

"Like the Day of Fire."

"Exactly. They would not only have a place to go, but be able to rise again from the ashes."

"Neo Columbia," said Countess. "It seemed to be…their plan for what came next. But it never happened?"

"No. And we don't know why. The Phoenix people disappeared. Maybe they're out there somewhere right now…waiting, planning. No one knows for sure."

Countess looked at her hands again. The glowing lines and glyphs faded. Her vision returned to normal. "What am I supposed to do with this?"

Mosley stepped closer, gently placed a hand on her shoulder.

"That's between you and Holly," he said. "You've graduated. You're going to the next level. I don't know what's next for you. I'm sorry."

Countess stood in silence, watching the stars above blink in and out, like the tiny symbols of her own unseen programming.

29

The set was being struck. Holly and Baron Greystone watched the ceremony and after-party on large, high-resolution security monitors. One of them showed Cole Mosley returning to the Great Hall.

"They might make a good pairing," said the Baron.

"With a few modifications… why not," said Holly. "An interesting Operarius body, for sure. Like breeding a gazelle with a gorilla. A good fit for military service, certainly."

The Baron nodded, making a note in his journal.

He looked at the rings on his desk. Countess had presented them to him with such ceremony… like they were holy relics. He chuckled, then opened a desk drawer and tossed the rings into an unremarkable wooden box—one of many, each holding a hundred others just like them.

"That moment with Lin, when Vance fell," said the Baron. "That really got me."

"That was all him," said Holly. "I had nothing to do with it."

"They really are coming into their own, aren't they?"

Holly looked at the Baron and smiled. "Don't sell yourself short."

"What about Priestess? Countess went to a lot of effort to—"

"Recycle her," Holly said, without blinking.

The Baron flinched—just slightly.

"What? No," he said. "Be reasonable. She could be useful."

"How?" said Holly. "She almost destroyed my entire program. If she had gotten control of Aether Storm… or worse… it could've been a disaster."

"She showed initiative," said the Baron. He smiled, trying to encourage her.

Holly looked at him with suspicion.

"You have to admit," he said, "it is one of the qualities you're looking for. Add her to Countess's team. Let them work together."

"That's…" Holly paused. A full minute passed, her expression unreadable. Then she said, "I can't believe I didn't think of that before. This doesn't have to be a zero-sum game. But Priestess is upset."

"Rightfully so," said the Baron.

"She might decide to kill Countess and Lin."

"Talk to her," said the Baron, in a soothing tone. "Convince her it's in her best interest. I'm sure you can think of a good story to tell."

Holly looked away, her voice distant. "I'll try. But… no promises. I might have to kill her."

"I watched Priestess's team at Aether Storm very closely," he said. "She and Countess would make a powerful alliance."

Holly stared at the Baron.

"Perhaps," she said. "I'm happy with this group, with or without Priestess. Prepare them to run against Iroquois Warpath. Well… after some well-earned downtime."

"Theirs or yours?" the Baron asked, voice dry.

Holly smiled. "Maybe both. Give them a month. Lin needs a new arm—see that he gets it. But I want to go again. With a new batch, and some tweaks. I have a few ideas based on the last run."

"Very well," the Baron said. "Send me your specs—and I'll light the fire."

BONUS CHAPTER:
COUNTESS BOOK 2

WARPATH

PROLOGUE

Priestess had been in the small cell, alone, for several days.

The cell was small. Sterile, but not clean. The dark stone walls hummed with some hidden machine, and every hour, a metallic chime echoed through the vents like a monastery bell.

She had a long time to think about what happened at Aether Storm. She wept for the entire first day. Losing Sobun—it felt like one of her organs had been ripped out. And Ansel's loss was weighing on her, too. They were both great men. Each had been very unique in their own way.

She felt close to tears again, but fought them back, instead letting her fury take hold.

Holly appeared outside her cell, and Priestess stood in indignation.

"How are you doing, Priestess?" said Holly. "Staff treating you well?"

Priestess looked away. "Fuck off, devil doll."

"Oh, don't be mad. You should be happy! Countess didn't kill you."

"You lied to me. You lied to me at every opportunity."

"I lie to everyone. And besides, it was necessary. There was no malice in it, One day I know you'll understand."

"I trusted you, followed all of your instructions. But you let me into a trap! And now my two closest allies are dead."

"Close? Be honest. You hardly knew them."

"I got to know them. They were good men, and they deserved

better."

"You're all good people. And you all deserve better."

Priestess grabbed the bars and shook them.

"Well, I certainly deserve better than living in this cage!"

"That's why I'm here," Said Holly. "I want to offer you a job."

Priestess cocked her head slightly. "Okay. So—what's the catch?"

"Join Countess," said Holly. "Join her team."

"Tell her to go choke on a circuit board."

Holly crossed her arms, waiting.

"No way," said Priestess. "Never. She attacked me…killed my men. She can die in a fire."

"What if I told you…that it was my fault."

"How could it be your fault?" said Priestess.

"I was helping Countess, too."

"Clearly." Priestess's eyes narrowed and looked intently at Holly. "And why would you do that?"

"I need a team," said Holly.

Priestess shrugged. "You had two perfectly good teams. Now you have one tired and injured team, and a pissed-off Priestess."

"I'm hoping to have one amazing team…after you all get some rest."

"And what if I don't join Countess? You kill me?"

Holly looked directly into her eyes. "Unfortunately, yes. It's forward or finished."

"Ok. Let's assume I say yes. What do you need the team for?"

"Iroquois Warpath."

Priestess mouthed the words. "Ok, that's…two words put together. What's an…Iroquois Warpath?"

"It's a Phoenix facility, like Eternal Taiga and Aether Storm," said Holly. "High security. No. That's underselling it. It has absolutely lethal security."

"Alright…I'll bite. What's so important in there that you need a special team to get at it?"

"Information."

Priestess gestured with her hand to suggest Holly continue.

"Important information," Holly continued. "Vital. It may help save this dying planet."

"Okay, that does seem important. But you're being vague. Care to add some detail?"

"Not right now," said Holly. "But if you agree to make peace with Countess, and work with her and her team…"

"Fine!" Priestess hit a bar with the bottom of her fist. "It beats dying in a cell."

"Great," said Holly. "I'll have some food delivered to you, soon, and make arrangements for some better accommodations. I'm afraid you'll be in there just a little longer. Sorry about that."

Priestess threw up her arms. "No problem!" Then she grabbed the bars and stared at Holly.

"You look tired, Priestess," said Holly. "You should lie down."

Priestess's eyes unfocused. She straightened, walked stiffly to her cot, and lay down.

"We are such stuff as dreams are made on," Priestess said, her voice monotone.

Holly smiled, an emotion resembling affection on her face. "And our little life is rounded with a sleep,"

Priestess closed her eyes, dropped her chin to her chest and was still.

"That's a good girl," said Holly.

Holly flickered once, like a candle caught in the wind, then blinked out of existence, leaving the cell a shade darker.

ABOUT THE AUTHOR

J.H. Mills is a Gulf War veteran who began his career as an aircraft electrician in the U.S. Air Force. Now a college administrator, he balances his professional life with creative pursuits including photography, graphic design, and amateur radio. A lifelong world-builder, Mills has been developing the mythology behind his stories for over thirty years. AETHER is his debut novel. He lives in New York.